# PARTY

# OF

# FOOLS

## Empire of Eats Novella #1

Cedar McCloud

ISBN-13: 978-1-958051-71-9

Published with the Kraken Collective
www.krakencollectivebooks.com

This book is dedicated to every favorite food I've ever had. Thank you for keeping me alive and comforting me when I needed it most!

# 1

## A Strange Stranger With a Stranger Appetite

Ale's Well That Ends Well was not the *seediest* bar in the Capital, but it was certainly up there on the list. There were not, on the whole, many murders there, despite its patrons' tendency to solve even minor problems with violence. For all its dim lighting and ramshackle appearance, it was kept surprisingly clean, and perhaps that was why its reputation hovered an inch above the metaphorical shit-filled gutters.

Gary, the owner and bartender, refused

to serve anyone who tromped in with mud on their boots. There was a boot scraper by the door for a reason, and a doormat, and anyone who neglected to use them would soon find themselves covered head-to-toe in filth as they were thrown out into the city streets. Gary was grizzled and beefy, a middle-aged human man who had slept drunkenly in his own share of alleyways. After he lost his leg in the war with Vertex, his mother had used her ill-gotten savings to buy the building. He was not about to let her sacrifice be disrespected.

Gary would never kick his own mother out of the bar, even if she came in with horse dung dripping from every limb. Gladys the Destroyer was sixty years old and, they said, in her prime. She had more battle scars than you could count, was six feet tall and taller with boots on, and had that lean, mean, wiry look that older folks get when all their fat melts away into muscle. Her right eye was missing, the empty socket covered by a patch, and she kept her long gray hair slicked back in a braid that doubled as a whiplash if she turned her head quickly enough.

In other words, Gladys was an

intimidating lady. Patrons of the bar gave her a nod or a salute if she was around—and she was always around these days, nursing a dark beer and glaring into the middle distance, preoccupied by conflicts long past. Why she was not out fighting, cheating, stealing, and doing all the things a woman of her class liked to do was a mystery.

Except to Reed. Reed was a halfling ten years Gladys's junior, fat and scruffy with graying stubble that constituted a full beard for someone of his kind. His clothes were finer than you might expect: silk doublets and embroidered waistcoats, but they were clearly old and worn, the relic of a more well-funded youth. There were mended patches and the silver thread in the embroidery was tarnished, much like Reed's once-black hair. His lined brown face wore an expression that might be mistaken for boredom, but was actually a calculated, patient calm.

He often provided casual entertainment at Ale's Well. On a typical evening, the bar was far too noisy and crowded to fully appreciate the sound of his lute or his pleasantly rough voice belting anti-establishment songs and poor-man's ballads. But if you came very early or very late, you might catch a tune without interference. You might think, *Where have I heard that voice before? It sounds familiar,* and you would be right. You probably had heard it before—but Reed would only shake his head and smile if you asked how that might be true.

Of course, if you came on *particular* nights of the month… you might just get a full dinner and a show. Reed might be in it, or he might be directing it, or someone else entirely might be in charge. You had to know how to get in, and you had to be trustworthy. Gladys, Reed, and their associates made sure of that.

They made for an odd pair of friends, the barbarian woman and the halfling musician. But they *were* friends.

"Can't you play somethin' that ain't depressing as a one-wheeled cart full of kittens down a dry well?" Gladys yelled as Reed finished his ballad with a heavy handed strum.

"Wouldn't it be more depressing if the well had water in it?" Reed replied, face as calm as ever. "Also, how's a cart fit down a well?"

"That ain't the point," Gladys said.

"It is if I'm to understand exactly where your tolerance for 'depressing' songs lies," said Reed. "It's a continuum, you know, a full spectrum of sadness. I need to know where your *point* lies on it so I know what to play and what not to play."

Gladys scoffed and pushed her empty mug toward Gary, who filled it without having to be asked. It was early evening, the dinner crowd not yet arrived, though they were certainly on their way. Gladys and Reed were the only two people in the bar aside from Old Kurt in the corner, and Old Kurt paid them no mind. He never paid anybody mind.

Reed adjusted himself on his stool, which sat on a small elevated platform to the left of the bar. It would have been too kind to call it a stage, given the lack of proper lighting or acoustics, let alone space. His knees were aching in a way that meant trouble was coming. Like leaves showing their silvery undersides as warm updrafts of air heralded a thunderstorm on the way.

"Look, Gladdy," he said, "you want to put

in a request? Toss me a coin, buy me a beer, treat me to a meal. You know the rules."

Gary, who had ducked into the kitchen to get the soup and bread and sausages going for dinner, stuck his shaved head back out with a scowl that was missing more than one tooth.

"Rules don't apply to Mama, she's the Lady of the—"

Reed cut him off with a wave of his hand. "Alright alright, I was just joking, don't get your shorts in a twist," he said, and then turned back to Gladys. "What'll it be, your Ladyship? Mrs. The Destroyer from the Hundred Mile Waste, Bandit Queen of the Banded Canyon, slayer of the High Road Highwayman?"

"I ain't no missus, never have been, never will be," Gladys snorted, "but you flatter me, you fool. Play me some of that *hard* stuff I know you done been workin' on. Like my ballad. You still workin' on my ballad, ain'tcha?"

"Mayhaps."

"Mayhaps my *ass*. Lemme hear it."

In another life, Reed was known for his honeyed vocals and three octave range. He still employed these skills in his work as a shady bar bard, but it was not what came to mind when people heard his name. What came to mind was the screaming. He didn't do it for every song, but you only had to hear it once for it to stick with you.

First-time listeners were shocked to hear such a deep, sonorous, shout come out of such a small and frumpy person. This was part of the draw, though Reed scream-sang not for the attention, but because, as he said, there was no other way to fully express the rage, frustration, and awe that lived in the vast, dark universe of his heart.

Gladys was used to it. Gladys understood. She listened with a smile on her thin lips and sipped her beer approvingly. This was why they were friends.

This was also when the Stranger entered the building. As a seedy bar, Ale's Well was used to strangers. They had what you might call a diverse clientèle, the sort who didn't ask questions and never gave easy answers when it came to who or what they were and which line of work they were in, exactly. It was fluid that way, a liminal space in which a person might become anyone or anything at all, no matter who they were on paper.

Unfortunately, liminality fit this Stranger like a corset two sizes too small. You could see the way their strongly defined character squeezed out in all the wrong places, from the set of their broad shoulders to the way their cloak swirled lyrically around their feet. Their boots were too expensive for this district despite having quite a bit of mud scraped from them before entering.

Reed and Gladys appeared not to notice the Stranger. There's a trope in stories like these where the hero walks into the seedy tavern and everyone stops to look at them, silence falling like an anvil. That may happen sometimes, somewhere, but not this day and not here.

Instead, Reed repeated the throaty chorus of Gladys's ballad, eyes squeezed shut, face tipped toward the sky. Gladys's eyes remained fixed on him, her foot tapping ever so slightly.

That's not to say the two of them didn't notice the Stranger clomp across the room and plop down, on the seat right beside Gladys. Not even a stool in between them for courtesy. They were simply too smart to let the Stranger *know* they were on to them. The only indication that something was wrong was the way Gladys's beer paused right below her lip, hovering unsipped.

"Hello, good Sir, Madam, or honored Friend!" the Stranger said to Gary in what was likely meant to be a real whisper, but came out as the stage variety instead.

The stage whisper should have been lost beneath Reed's singing. Instead it cut a channel through the melodic screaming like hot water through butter. Gary responded with a tilt of his head. Gladys's beer moved farther from her mouth.

The Stranger was handsome, perhaps even beautiful. She had a face that was all smooth, strong angles, with cheekbones high enough to build a defensive fort on. Her skin was the warm brown of perfectly steeped tea lit by a sunbeam, her voluminous black hair done into twists, partially pulled back above the ears. The ears themselves were laden with jewelry which, were it real gold, might earn the wearer a club over the head in this part of town.

Gary didn't think anyone would club this person. Beneath a white linen tunic, her arms bulged with muscle. The shoulders they attached to were so broad as to be comical. Gary stopped thinking about his Favorite Employee hidden beneath the bar (a bat with nails in it) and decided it was in his best interest to play nice.

"What can I do y'for?" Gary asked in his best Customer Service voice, which was only a little less gruff than his usual.

The Stranger steepled her fingers thoughtfully. She pursed her full lips, then grinned and shrugged. The grin was meant to be casual, but the force of its charm pushed Gary back from the counter. Gladys put her beer down.

"Would you happen to have—I mean, you got a house special? Drink of course, but food, too, if it's not too early," the Stranger said.

Gary puffed out his chest. His regulars didn't know the meaning of 'house special,' but he had one all right. From the bar he retrieved the cleanest glass he owned, which was only a *little* dusty, and filled it from a bottle whose label might have been considered vulgar in certain company. It had a squirrel on it in a compromising position and a pun on the word 'nuts' in the name, which Gary thought to be the highest echelon of humor. He couldn't help a snicker as he set the deep brown ale with its frothy white top in front of the Stranger.

"Just a mo' on the grub," Gary said. "Don't go downing that all'n one go. It's a sipper, that one. Strong stuff."

The Stranger picked up the glass and toasted it in Gary's direction. "Understood, my good man. I trust your judgment."

Gary beamed and headed into the kitchen, rubbing his calloused hands together in delight. It had been quite a while since he felt appreciated by anyone other than his mother, especially when it came to cooking.

Said mother had been slowly turning in her seat for the past few minutes, so as not to alert the Stranger to her interest. Reed, his knees sensing that trouble had indeed arrived, finished the ballad three verses early and set his lute to the side with a bow. Over in the corner, Old Kurt continued to pickle silently. No one paid him any mind.

The Stranger raised her glass to Reed,

then set it down so she could, of all things, applaud. Vigorously. Reed was not so easily flattered as Gary, but he pretended to be, bowing again with added flourish. He held out a battered cap and the Stranger produced a silver coin, which she flicked expertly into the center of the hat.

"Don't think I've heard music like that before," the Stranger said. "So intense! What do you call it?"

Reed shrugged. "Hard to put a name to the purest expression of one's soul," he said. "If you've got suggestions, I'm all ears."

He tugged on one ear, which was a sign to Gladys to play it cool. Reed wasn't sure she saw it; her one eye was fixed on the Stranger. He hopped down from the stage and took the seat on the other side of the newcomer, albeit slowly. The ache in his knees had gone unpleasantly tingly. At least Gary had the decency to pick chairs with rungs on them so the Little Folk could climb up. With his wooden leg, Gary was more sensitive than most to the plight of inaccessible furniture.

The thing was, Reed recognized the Stranger. He had to stop himself from staring, as shocked as he was, but there was no mistaking her for anyone else. The Stranger did not seem to recognize Reed, and for that he was... grateful.

Reed held out his hand and the Stranger took it. Her grip was firm and warm. "I'm Reed Thorley. Haven't seen you 'round here before...?" He let his voice trail off into a question.

"Val," said Emperor Consort Vallora the Undying Hero. "Yes, let's go with that. You can call me Val."

It was not unusual for someone to give a pseudonym in Ale's Well That Ends Well, but the would-be impostors were usually a bit more clever about their choices. Reed stared at Vallora's straight white teeth and wondered if the Emperor was playing a joke, if it was all *meant* to be transparent as a clean windowpane. It was impossible to tell.

"Pleasure to meet you, Val," Reed replied. "Welcome to the pub."

# 2

## A Royal Jerk, and Some Jerky

When Vallora did not appear for breakfast, Captain Andromeda suspected there would be trouble. When she entered the royal bed chambers through the enormous gilded mahogany doors (having first knocked politely, of course) and found the room empty, she *knew* that there would be trouble. And when she found the note pinned to Vallora's red silk pillow, she understood that the scope of said trouble was far beyond any shenanigans the Emperor had gotten into in recent decades. Centuries, even.

That this quest might rival the one in which Vallora and the Party saved the world nine hundred years ago did not cross Andromeda's mind. Likely because even to Andromeda, an elf approaching her one-hundred-ninetieth birthday, that was the stuff of legends.

Also, she was hungry. She wasn't allowed to start eating until Vallora did, and so her own breakfast sat on the lower garden balcony untouched. It was difficult to take in the full scope of the situation when her mind was squarely fixated on flaky pastries and hot sausages. She would have to break decorum.

"So help me, your Highness," she muttered to herself as she ate faster than was recommended for good digestion, "you'd better not have left the city by now."

For the past three decades, Vallora had insisted Andromeda call her by the nickname 'Lora,' but Andromeda had yet to let the appellation pass her lips. It wasn't proper or respectful, two qualities she held in enormously high regard. Especially when applying those qualities to herself.

It did not occur to Andromeda that refusing a request made by the Emperor, whatever that request was, might constitute disrespect in itself. No one was bold enough to tell her this, fearing not retribution, but what such a contradiction might do to Andromeda's orderly mind

This steadfast adherence to her own principles was, though Andromeda didn't know it, one of the reasons Vallora liked her so much.

The sausages sitting heavy in her stomach, Andromeda began with a methodical canvassing of the castle, making sure to check the back passageways used by the servants and staff. She tried to look casual while she did it, but Andromeda was not a casual person. The other inhabitants of Zenith Castle gave her a wide berth when they saw the ferocity of her scowl and heard her stomping down the wide stone corridors.

Occasionally she risked asking someone if they'd seen Vallora. Not enough people to cause a panic; word got around fast when it came to the castle staff. Andromeda didn't want a soul to know something unsavory was afoot if there was still a chance she could solve things herself.

Not a one of them had seen the Hero since last night, though she suspected the cook of lying. Mrs. Janey always grinned crookedly when she was covering for someone, which was often. Mrs. Janey was like a mother hen not just to the staff but to Vallora as well. She had a soft spot for someone who ate double portions for every meal and always ended with exuberant compliments to the chef.

Well, so much for that. The grounds were next.

Castle Zenith was a fortress, really, ringed by a wall ten stories high and as thick as a house. Between the wall and the castle were the royal hunting grounds, a thick and ancient forest with trees so gnarled they seemed to have wrinkled, wicked faces; they seemed, sometimes, as if they were alive. In a *sapient* way. It gave Andromeda the creeps, and she was an *elf* for Hero's sake. Elves *loved* trees.

This was when she discovered that the Dog had not left with Vallora, as expected. Andromeda supposed that other than Vallora's wife, the Empress, the Dog was the Emperor's closest friend in the entire world. The Dog, called Destiny, or 'Dez' by her guardian, was also nine hundred years old. Everyone swore she could speak, but in thirty-plus years, Andromeda had never heard her do so. Vallora insisted it was just a rumor.

Andromeda found Destiny laying despondently beside an old hunting shack on the east side of the grounds, splayed out as if she had been turned into a fur rug. She was a Credence shepherd, a big black and brown dog with pointy ears and a shaggy tail. Age, which had caught up with her before she became immortal, streaked her muzzle and back with silver, but she was as fit as a puppy. She thumped her tail twice as Andromeda approached, gazing up at her with big, sad brown eyes.

For the first time that morning, Andromeda felt a sense of triumph. If anyone could help track down Vallora, it was Destiny. The question was: would the Dog would feel too loyal to Vallora to foil her plans, or would being left out of them compel her to find the Hero and join in?

You wouldn't think a dog was capable of such complex reasoning, but Destiny was absolutely not a normal dog.

Andromeda knelt on the ground and

patted Destiny's soft head, giving her a scratch behind the ears for good measure. Dogs, even magical immortal ones, were so much easier to deal with than people—be they human, elf, dwarf, satyr, or whatever. Destiny thumped her tail again and raised her head for chin scratches.

"Hi, Destiny," she said. "Do *you* know where Emperor Vallora is?"

The Dog glanced away and stopped wagging her tail, for all the world like she was guiltily hiding the answer. Andromeda reached into one of the many pockets on her utility belt and pulled out a piece of jerky. Destiny's eyes snapped back.

"She went out on an adventure, didn't she?" Andromeda said, wiggling the jerky back and forth. "Without bringing along anyone who cares about her safety! Not even you, and you're her best friend. How about we go find her, hm?"

Andromeda bit off a piece of jerky for herself and offered the rest to Destiny, who swallowed it without chewing. The dog looked up hopefully, her eyes darting to the pouch and back. Destiny was smart enough to open the snaps if she wanted, but she was polite, at least with people she liked and knew well.

Andromeda took out another piece—she always carried dried meat and other small, dense foodstuff, both for afternoon snacks and in case of a siege or other unexpected emergency—and offered it to Destiny in a closed fist.

"What do you say?"

Destiny scrambled to her feet and barked twice. Then she sat primly and put her paw on Andromeda's hand.

"I'll take that as a yes."

Andromeda opened her hand and Destiny gently took the meat before once again tossing it down her gullet without chewing. Then she turned, and with a glance back to make sure Andromeda was following, headed off through the woods.

# 3

## The Subtle Flavor of Subterfuge

The two friends watched in silence as Vallora picked up her beer and took a first, cautious sip. She closed her eyes and swirled it around her mouth before swallowing, throat bobbing and long eyelashes fluttering just a bit.

"Mmmm," she said in a smooth, drawn out noise of satisfaction. "Rich, sweet, warm. Notes of caramel and rye. Nutty. Hazelnut? No. Almond? Hm. Not walnut...."

Reed leaned his grizzled cheek into one hand. "Think it's acorn," he said.

Vallora opened her eyes and produced another dazzling smile. The only reason it didn't knock Reed off his seat was that as a chunky halfling, Reed had quite a low center of gravity.

"Acorn!" repeated Vallora. "Brilliant! Though, I thought acorns were poisonous."

"Not if y'soak em first," Reed said. "Been kind of a resurgence in their popularity lately. Are you new in town? Or just from the other side of it?"

He laughed and slapped his knee. Zenith was an urban monstrosity larger than some countries. Some *former* countries, since practically all of them were now under the most civil rule of the Unending Empire.

It had also been magically raised into the sky nine hundred years ago and deposited in its current geographical position by none other than Vallora herself, supposedly to save the city from utter destruction.

"Suppose I am," said Vallora, and took another sip of her beer, eyebrows raised.

Reed wondered whether Zenith Castle counted as 'outside of town' or 'the other side,' given how isolated it was in its circling walls. Perhaps that was the joke. Reed had been inside the Castle, once upon a time. A lifetime ago for him, but certainly only yesterday to the immortal Hero.

Yet Vallora showed no sign of recognizing Reed's face—or his voice. Maybe you didn't bother to remember peasants when you were royalty. Maybe you had people to do that for you.

There didn't seem to be any Royal Guardsmen about. No clanking armor outside, just increasingly worrisome clanking from the kitchen, where Gary was making his *house special*. Gladys had a sixth sense for law enforcement and would have been down the cellar and out the back tunnel before you could so much as say, "Open up!" No, for some reason, Vallora was alone. *Un*guarded.

"Well!" said Reed, "Always glad to see a new face about! New ears, too. Most nights the only one who cares to toss me a coin is my old mate Gladys, here."

He gestured at Gladys, whose unblinking stare had not ceased throughout the entire conversation, even while drinking her beer. She set her now-empty glass down on the counter (on a coaster of course; she might be a barbarian, but this was Gary's place and Gary required everyone use one) with a hollow *thunk*. Gary scrambled out of the kitchen, refilled his mother's drink, and hurried back in, though not without flashing Vallora a double thumbs-up.

Vallora returned the gesture enthusiastically, then looked to Gladys, whose eye narrowed with suspicion.

"Not Gladys the Destroyer?" Vallora said, in a tone of mild disbelief and admiration. "Lady from the Hundred Mile Waste, Bandit Queen of the Banded Canyon, Slayer of the High Road Highwayman?"

Gladys did not move a single taught muscle. "Depends on who's askin', don't it?"

Vallora held up two gloved hands in a gesture of peace. The gloves were plain and ordinary, which made it extra clear that they hadn't seen a day of work in their likely short lifetime.

"*I'm* not asking for trouble, that's for sure," said Vallora.

*No*, thought Reed, *you ARE the trouble.*

Gladys sniffed. "'Bout time someone's

dang heard of me b'sides my own enemies. Do you know how many assassination attempts I done survived? Were I the trusting sort, I tell ya, I wouldn'ta got a story and a half for each of 'em."

She glowered, her scarred countenance a mask of fury that would have most scurrying away from her as quickly as possible. Vallora only grinned and clapped her hands together.

"I," she said, "would *love* to hear one."

At that moment, Gary came back carrying a giant plate of what must, given the circumstances, be food. He set it down in front of Vallora and topped off the nut ale with the confidence of a much younger, less traumatized man. The man he had been before the war, Gladys noted, her attention finally drawn away from the Emperor.

"There y'are, friend, one house special!" he said, and stood back to admire his work.

There was definitely bread in there, and beans, and chunks of the cheapest end of the pig, or maybe cow. There were black bits which might have once been onions, green stuff that might be parsley, and red sauce that was definitely spicy, given that the steam wafting off it made everyone's eyes water.

Vallora gave it an appraising look that Reed thought belonged in one of those fancy Upper Circumference joints, not a back alley bar. In his former life, he had eaten at places like that. Everything came in small portions, painstakingly prepared by at least three chefs, with a full list of nameable ingredients and their origins. Surely that was the sort of food Vallora was used to.

Still, she raised her fork and knife with a gleeful expression. She took one bite, chewed thoughtfully, swallowed, and took another. The bliss in Vallora's dark eyes made Gladys wonder if her son had missed his calling as a cook. Gladys didn't have any tastebuds to speak of and had always assumed that Gary's cooking was a notch above the slop served in surrounding local establishments, if only because she was his mother, and that's what she ought to think. She was now thinking there might be more to it than that.

Vallora inhaled half the plate before looking cheerfully up at Gary and saying, "Fantastic! Authentic! This is the sort of stuff that'll put some hair on your chest."

"And it ain't got no hairs *in* it, neither," Gary said proudly.

"You, ah, a food critic? Work for one of those restaurant directory catalogs?" Reed asked. Gary shot him an astonished look, having never considered such things existed. His worldview was suddenly expanding.

Vallora shook her head, the shells on the ends of her twists clacking together. "Oh no, just someone who loves to eat. This is just one of many stops on the continental food tour I have planned. Starting here, of course. No food like that of your hometown!"

"Ain't grub pretty much the same everywhere?" Gladys asked. "Why go to all that trouble?"

Vallora dabbed her mouth with a notably clean handkerchief, produced from a cloak pocket. Ale's Well did *not* have napkins, though Gary would soon discover them as he explored the concept of fine dining in the coming months.

"I've been a bit cooped up lately, you see. Struck by a bit of wanderlust, and a lot of appetite," Vallora said. "Surely an esteemed woman such as yourself understands the urge to be on the road, out under the stars, visiting foreign lands and experiencing all they have to offer?"

Gladys had to concede to that. "Aye. There was a time when I—"

Reed interrupted her before she could get going. "Excuse us for a second," he said, slipping off his stool and motioning for Gladys to join him. "I think I've gotten a bit hungry myself. Don't trouble yourself, Gary my old boy, we'll serve ourselves and then have story time with… Val."

Vallora nodded, mouth full of beans and bread and bits, and gave him a friendly little wave. Reed smiled. He'd had a lot of practice, in both this life and the former, of putting on a smile while screaming internally. Vallora was the immortal embodiment of the Empire and all its mythology. He hoped that for all her power, she could not see through his guise.

Reed and Gladys went into the kitchen, which was its own barrage of smells and bubbling gloopy sounds. Gladys picked up the ladle from the pot of house special, took a gulp, and smacked her lips appreciatively.

Reed kept his voice low. “Gladdy, you understand who that is out there, don’t you?”

Gladys took another gulp of house special. “Some young whippersnapper with money playin’ at adventure. You wanna bet how long before they come to a bad end? How much?”

“You always fix those bets,” Reed replied grumpily.

“Heh,” said Gladys. “Yeah, I do.”

“No,” Reed continued, his voice sharp. “That out there, I swear to you on the Whispering Stones, is Vallora the Undying Hero. You know, the Emperor Consort? The Savior of—”

Gladys twisted her head to see through the heavy canvas that served as the kitchen’s door. Reed smacked her on the arm (it was like smacking a metal post and made his palm smart) but she only craned her long neck farther.

“That ain’t Vallora,” she said.

“How do you know?” Reed asked, folding his arms.

“Not tall enough.”

Now Reed craned his neck to look through the crack. He’d put Vallora at just under six feet tall, and he was pretty good at heights. He rolled his eyes, and Gladys untwisted herself to look at him again.

"Look," he said, "back in my old life, I met her once."

Gladys raised one thin gray eyebrow.

Reed harumphed and waved his hands in the air between them. "It was a whole thing. We were there to, you know. The show had gotten so popular with the nobles that the royal couple wanted their own viewing..."

Gladys's one eye narrowed. She loomed over Reed, who was standing on a crate of onions, the closest thing to a vegetable that Gary would allow inside his kitchen.

"You swear it? That's *her*?" she asked in a deadly whisper.

Reed nodded. "Been thirty years, but she looks the same as I remember. *Exactly* the same."

"I thought they've been keepin' the Emperor outta public eye," Gladys said, "on account of, y'know."

"People like us?" Reed said dryly.

"I was gonna say our *friends*. What in the seven hells is she doing down here, then?" Gladys said. She blinked and stood up tall, glancing around suspiciously. "Is this a trap?"

"Do you think it is?"

Gladys stilled, thinking. Or rather, feeling. Her sense for law enforcement had prevented more than one plot and several ambushes in the past. When asked how exactly it worked, she said she didn't know, but thought it had something to do with the bit of Watch baton stuck in her right thigh. She took another sip of house special.

"Hmm. Naw. Yer knees hurt?" she asked.

Reed nodded. "They're practically numb, now. I think… Vallora might be here of her own accord. You heard what she said about feeling *cooped up* and wanting the open road and all that. Makes sense. Suppose being immortal would get boring after a few centuries."

Gladys made a face that said she more or less agreed. "So, what do we do? Think we can take 'er?" She smacked a bony fist into her palm meaningfully.

"No, no, this isn't the time for muscle. This is the time for subterfuge," Reed said.

"For what? Is that some kind of new

potion or poison?" asked Gladys. "Poison's the coward's way out."

Reed thought that if Vallora wasn't immune to poison, it would probably take ten times the usual dose to knock the Hero out, much less kill her. Not that he wanted to *kill* Vallora. Lots of people did, but Reed had other ideas about serving up justice.

"What I mean is," he said, "we play along. Get friendly, ask to join the party. What's a meal without friends? And maybe along the way… on this continental food tour or whatever it is… we steer Vallora straight to *them*. No struggle! And no poison."

"Ah," said Gladys. "A trick!"

# 4

## Again?

Destiny, who'd had her nose to the ground for hours now, suddenly looked up, whined, and bounded off down a narrow side street. Andromeda followed grimly, mentally rehearsing how to scold Vallora in a way that was firm but appropriate given their social standing.

It was about time. Andromeda had written and rewritten the speech several times now in her head, and the drafts were starting to muddle. She hadn't had a proper lunch, only more jerky, half of which she gave to the Dog. Now it was going on teatime and hunger was lending a darker color to her words.

Destiny barked, and Andromeda rounded the corner. The buildings in the Lower Circumference were narrow and stacked stories high, lives overflowing their tiny rooms into whatever street or alleyway lay beyond. She skirted a precarious pile of used chamberpots and another of loose compost (the two were, of course, related).

Andromeda was born in a place like this. Her parents were refugees from the war in Jubilee, but they'd worked their way into the Middle Circumference by the time she was in her fifties. She remembered clearly those early years crammed together in tiny rooms, eating the vegetables the neighbor grew in old boots nailed to the windowsill, making newspaper cutout dolls for the children, and practicing her swordsmanship with a broom handle.

It hadn't been all that bad, so long as they had food for the week. And that it didn't rain, given that their ceiling leaked. Her parents were quick to remind her that they had more than some people.

Andromeda realized that Destiny had

led her to an orphanage. There were *many* children without parents in the City of Hours, and most of them came from wars abroad. The Empire might have saved their nations from one despot or another, but there was always a civilian death toll. The least they could do was bring the kids back here and try to find them loving families.

She'd once asked why they couldn't avoid so many civilian casualties in the first place; she was told that was just the cost of war. She asked why they couldn't find the children families in their countries of origin, where the land and culture were familiar; she was told that damaged infrastructure and lack of resources weren't conducive to raising orphans. Who would take on the burden of adopting them when the whole country was shattered and rebuilding?

Andromeda hadn't known what to say to that. It *seemed* logical, but still, she felt a pang of unease as she approached the run-down brick building. Framing the door were garden boxes made from old crates, brimming with wildflowers and weeds. The exterior brick walls were caked with layers of colorful paint, some of it fresh, some of it faded. The newest mural depicted a sunrise on one side of the door and a sunset on the other, with lopsided buildings and trees made from green handprints.

The handprints were so *tiny*. It had been a long time since Andromeda was around children.

Destiny sat down in front of the door and barked. Someone opened it.

"Dez? What are you doing—oh, Captain," said a brown-haired human man, glancing up at her.

He saluted and opened the door wider; another face poked out, saluting as well. Andromeda stopped in her tracks, desperately trying to match their faces with names.

Andromeda was decently faceblind. To compensate, she memorized details about how people wore their hair, their taste in clothing, or their scent. When it came to the Guard, she was used to recognizing the little quirks of their armor: the chips and dents, the scratches, the regard or disregard for dress code regulations. These two were in plainclothes, which meant they were undercover for some reason.

*Oh no*, she thought, *they're with the Empress.*

Andromeda gestured for them to be at ease. "Well met," she said, and left the greeting hanging over an extremely awkward silence as she did not address either of them by name.

Andromeda might have learned to recognize them in plainclothes if the other guards ever invited her out for casual drinking, gaming, and the like. That had only happened once or twice before she became Captain, and never afterward. For years she told herself it was normal for the enlisted and even the officers to exclude their superiors—who wants to drink with their boss?

Then she'd found out that they treated Commander Haywood, *her* superior and Empress Tansy's personal bodyguard like he was one of them. Like a *friend.*

*If Tansy is here, then so is Haywood,* she thought. *Shit.*

What if Vallora was here, as well? That didn't seem likely, but perhaps Tansy had run into her wife before Andromeda managed to track her down. That would be a massive embarrassment, but at least

Vallora would be safe.

"How goes… the day?" Andromeda tried to come up with a way to ask if Vallora was inside without a) revealing that she was missing or b) having to go inside, where Empress Tansy and Commander Haywood were undoubtedly waiting.

The two guards stared at her. The brown-haired one knelt to pet Destiny, who was sniffing around his pockets for treats. Destiny might be immortal and literate, but she was still a *dog*.

The other guard had brown hair as well, in the same short regulation cut. They were significantly curvier than their partner, at least, so there was that to tell them apart. They glanced inside, then back at Andromeda.

"Same old, Captain," they said cautiously. "*She's* visiting orphans to keep their spirits up, healing the sick ones, donating some big bags of silver, the usual."

"Something we can assist you with, Ma'am?" asked the other guard. "Do you need to see *her*?"

Before Andromeda could answer, there was a high-pitched squeal from inside the orphanage.

"PUPPY!"

A tsunami of children burst through the narrow doorway and into the street with a crash of delighted laughter and a frothing of hands. Destiny bore the onslaught with dignity as the orphans patted her, grabbed her tail, and climbed on her back. One enterprising young halfling even licked Destiny's face and barked. Destiny barked back, and the children scattered in surprise.

They were all no more than four or five years old, Andromeda guessed, though she was nearly as bad at ages as she was recognizing faces. She assumed the older children were at school—or work. She knew from experience that in this part of town, once your age hit double digits, you usually were expected to get a job.

At this point, Empress Tansy appeared, a baby in her arms—definitely an orphan, given the Empress and Emperor had no children of their own. The Empress looked at Destiny, blinked in recognition, and then looked up at Andromeda. Their eyes met, widening with equal surprise. Andromeda was the first to look away. She tried not to flinch.

Empress Tansy Tasmin Albina Rose, Healer of the World, was largely held to be the most beautiful woman on the planet—and the kindest. She was of average height, with a willowy figure and a pale oval face that shone like the moon to Vallora's sun. Her brown eyes were large and downturned, always glossy as if on the verge of tears. But she kept a soft smile on her lips to reassure all that she was *fine*, thank you very much.

"Captain Stagge," Tansy said in her high, gentle voice, "fancy meeting you here!"

Andromeda stood at attention, bowed, saluted, and kept her gaze pinned firmly to the space between Tansy's delicate eyebrows. This way it would seem like she was making eye contact without actually having to do so. All eyes were intense to Andromeda, but Tansy's especially so.

"Good afternoon, your Highness," Andromeda said stiffly. "Pleasure to be in your presence! Do you require any assistance?"

"Oh, I'm fine," Tansy said. She bounced the baby on her hip, and it giggled.

"Lieutenant Smith and Officer Lane are here with me, and Commander Haywood is wrapping things up with the orphanage."

She nodded at the two Royal Guards in plainclothes. Tansy herself was dressed modestly, in a blue dress and slippers, her famously long brown hair braided up under a scarf. Tansy favored a perfume that was supposed to smell like her namesake, but to Andromeda it was all alcohol and dandelions. This signature scent was currently overcome by the stench of the Lower Circumference gutters.

Andromeda glanced over Tansy's shoulder and saw Commander Haywood lurking deeper inside the building; he was *not* undercover. He was dressed in the same floral surcoat and armor she wore. Yellow tansy and red roses intertwined. It was supposed to represent Tansy and Vallora, respectively, but 'Rose' was a surname that Vallora picked up from her wife when they got married. Less representative of Tansy and Vallora, more representative of... Tansy and Tansy. The design choice irked her.

Andromeda was glad Haywood was busy

right now. It was harder to refrain from punching him when she was hungry.

Destiny wandered back to Andromeda, tail wagging and tongue lolling. A couple of small children still clung to her fur with their sticky hands. Andromeda narrowed her eyes at the Dog. This was not how their day was supposed to go.

"Is Lora with you?" Tansy asked, her face brightening at the prospect.

"No, your Highness," Andromeda said automatically, and belatedly added, "We are... looking for her, though, Destiny and myself. Ma'am."

Smith and Lane exchanged pained glances. Andromeda was feared for her honesty, especially when directed at the royal couple. Sometimes the effect radius was so large that it affected (presumably) innocent bystanders. They'd heard the rumblings in the Castle this morning, and Vallora hadn't showed up for the sparring practice she often held with the Royal Guard. Something was definitely amiss, but why go and *say* so? To *Tansy* of all people?

A silence fell between them. A *royal* silence, which dampened the sound of the children, the nearby vendors hawking wares, and the workers on their tea breaks from the tannery or the mill or the ironworks, places where the only thing louder than people's voices was the stench.

"You… don't know where Lora is, Captain?" Tansy asked, and stopped rocking the orphan baby. The baby drooled. "Is everything all right?"

"Um," said Andromeda, who hadn't planned *this* conversation ahead of time. Not that her conversations with Tansy ever went as planned. "It's not *not* all right. Not yet. The Emperor left a note—"

She fumbled the paper from one of her many belt pouches and handed it to Tansy. Tansy gave the baby over to Lane and took the note. It read, in surprisingly plain handwriting:

*Gone to Lunch!*

*Just kidding. Sort of. Tansy, Captain, Commander, Council members, lovely castle staff, Dez the Bestest Girl in All the World, and whoever else it may concern: I'm very sorry, but I just can't take it anymore. I asked nicely many times over the last three decades to be let out of the Castle, but instead the door was further barred. Literally! Extra locks on all the doors! For my own safety, I've been told, but I'm afraid being so confined has left me in danger of losing my mind.*

*I just need some fresh air for a bit. Some road under my feet and stars over my head. I promise I'll be careful and won't let any silly rebels catch me. I'm the Hero, remember? Whatever happens, I'll always come back home in the end, where I belong. I will think of you all fondly! And to Tansy in particular: I think some space will be good for both of us.*

*Signed,*
*Emperor Vallora Grace Leontyne Rose, the Undying Hero*

"Oh dear," said Tansy, "not this again."

"Again?" echoed Andromeda.

Smith and Lane looked at one another. At least Andromeda could be counted on to say what they *wanted* to, but didn't dare.

Tansy motioned for them to herd the children back inside. Once they had, she cast a Circle of Silence to keep out prying eyes and ears. Anyone happening by their little group would suddenly find themselves wandering elsewhere, mentally or physically.

Tansy's big droopy eyes misted with nostalgia. She smiled wryly. "Lora wasn't born noble, you know. Well, we don't *know* the sort of bloodline she was born to, because she was a foundling, but her adoptive parents were poor farmers living just outside the Capital—the part we'd call the Rim, now. This place was... so much smaller then."

"Mm," said Andromeda, who had seen some of that expansion take place, both in the Capital and the wider Empire. It was like slime mold, multiplying itself exponentially in a weird living fractal. It ate everything in its path.

"Young Lora was so uncouth and funny and provincial," said Tansy. "That's why we became friends, even before she was the Hero."

Unbeknownst to the public, Vallora and Tansy's marriage was one of convenience, not romantic love. On their original quest to save the world, they'd become close friends, and afterward agreed to marry because, well, that was what people expected. Everyone knew that the Hero and the Princess were meant to be *together*, in that very particular way.

So, the two of them played along for the good of the Empire and the morale of its citizens. Andromeda was scandalized when she discovered the truth, but over time she was comforted by the fact that this was *also* a trope common to royal stories. Tansy had a secret lover among the nobility, and everyone was apparently fine with that, including Vallora.

Vallora currently had no one. Andromeda often wondered about that.

Tansy continued: "I think that young commoner is still inside—Lora's never fully taken to being royalty, even after all these centuries. Every couple hundred years, she gets the urge for adventure and just—runs away!"

Tansy laughed, which confused Andromeda. She didn't see anything funny about the situation. Especially considering the rebels had become more active of late, kidnapping nobles, threatening Council members, and distributing an alarming amount of Antihero propaganda.

They'd already attacked Vallora once and almost succeeded; only Tansy's immediate intervention had kept Vallora from dying. It was past time the rebels tried their secret weapon again. Andromeda felt a cold sting of panic at the thought of Vallora wounded or worse—not just because it would mean she failed at her job, but because… well…

She drummed her fingers on her gauntlet to soothe herself. "What did you do when it happened before?" Andromeda asked.

"Oh, we always catch Lora before she gets too far," Tansy said. "*Discreetly*, of course, so as not to cause a panic. That's how you're handling it now, am I right, Captain? Discreetly?"

Andromeda breathed a mental sigh of relief. "Yes, Your Highness. We've been tracking her all morning through a series of bakeries and cafés, just myself and Destiny. I do believe we're close."

She patted Destiny on the head and the Dog licked her fingers. *I'd be closer if I wasn't standing here talking to Tansy*, Andromeda thought, *but at least I know this has happened before. Everything's going to be all right.*

# 5

## It's Cheese O'Clock Somewhere

After finishing his plate of Gary's house special, Reed turned to Vallora and asked, "How do you feel about cheese and other assorted dairy products?"

"Strongly!" Vallora replied.

"Good," said Reed. "I know a place."

Of the many races and localities on the planet, Revel halflings enjoyed the most recognition and notoriety when it came to the handling of dairy. Revel was one of the first nations to be adopted into the Empire after its founding, seeing as it neighbored the Capital and produced much of its food.

It was largely plains and prairie, rolling farmland with soil made rich by tidal floodplains.

It didn't flood anymore, not since the building of the Solstice Dam two centuries earlier, and so much of the land which previously supported grain crops had been converted to dairy. What land *could* support crops was now mostly used to feed the animals.

Reed would know. He was born there, in what they called the Sea of Wheat and Hay.

Much of the Capital's populace originally hailed from somewhere else. Communities formed within the Rings based on those shared histories, cultures, and bloodlines. So it was that Reed was on friendly terms with most of the shopkeeps on Curd Street, which hosted the Capital's densest population of Revelers. Mostly halflings, but a good bit of humans and the occasional elf, as well. All with the genetic memory of dirt under their fingernails and bright sun on their faces.

Cheddar Luck Next Time was an unassuming building made from straw and mud brick, which kept the place cool in the muggy capital summer and warm in its snowy, gray winters. It boasted a large picture window which even the most snot-nosed ruffians didn't dare break or splatter with eggs—not unless they wanted to be banned from the premises of the best cheese shop in Zenith.

The shop's wooden sign swayed noiselessly in the wind. It was always well-oiled, as were the hinges of the front door. A string of tinny bells rang as Reed entered, with Vallora just behind. Gladys was bringing up the rear, keeping an eye out for trouble. No one had accosted them on the walk over, though Vallora had drawn a few curious stares. Less than Gladys expected, to be honest.

But then, the Undying Hero had been out of the public eye for some thirty years now. Anyone under forty might not even know what the Emperor *looked* like outside of artist's renderings, which, Gladys thought now that she had met the real thing, failed to capture the absurdly ordinary, good-natured charm of Vallora's face.

Vallora inhaled deeply as they entered Cheddar Luck Next Time and was clearly pleased by its unique funk. Those who were sensitive to scents, like dear Andromeda, wouldn't have cared for it—but it was not a *bad* smell, despite the reputation held by fermented foods. It was earthy, sharp, grounding, and tangy all at once. It was the smell of *culture.*

Reed gestured grandly at the shop's tidy, well-lit interior. "Here we are! The best cheesemonger in the Capital," he said.

"Don't you mean, best in the Empire?" came a voice from the back of the room, low and amused. "Or have you been seeing other cheese shops behind my back, Mr. Thorley?"

Karsten stepped out from behind the counter, dressed in simple earth-toned clothes and a clean apron embroidered with the name of the shop. They were a halfling of Reed's age, early fifties, with long black hair, medium brown skin, and sharp gray eyes behind a pair of round spectacles. Which they now peered over in mock-reproach at Reed.

"Ah, sorry, slip of the tongue," Reed responded. "You know, my new companion here was telling me that she's tried cheeses and yogurts and such all over the world, so she might actually be able to confirm that title for you."

"Happy to be of service," Vallora said, giving Karsten a little salute, "and to pay for the experience, of course."

Karsten chuckled and rubbed their hands together thoughtfully. "No, no, I'll be the one serving *you* today. I'll whip up a nice sample board for you—feel free to browse in the meantime."

Karsten ducked behind the counter and got busy. The counter itself was a curious but not uncommon setup in big cities, with a shorter end for Little Folk and a higher end for Taller Folk, which Karsten would access via stepstool. A glass case in front of each displayed a number of popular wares which could be sliced and sold by the pound.

The rest of the room was open to accommodate waiting customers. A few shelves sold packaged goods that went well with cheese, like dried meats, jellies, jams, and crackers. Everything was neatly packaged in brown paper and labeled by hand in a flowing script.

Off to the side, there were a couple of small round tables, carefully selected to accommodate patrons who varied in height. Two porthole windows dropped sunbeams onto the seating area, and fed an array of hanging green vines. It was all rather quaint.

It was also a common meeting place for members of the resistance. The resistance had good opinions about cheese, generally speaking. Though when drunk or bored, any topic could become grounds for intense debate.

The trio took their seats, glancing at one another in silence as each waited for someone else to begin speaking.

Eventually, Vallora slapped the table rhythmically with her hands and said, "So! What do you two do for work?"

Gladys shrugged. "I'm retired."

"From banditry and destroying?" Vallora asked.

"Let's call it politics and mercenary work," Reed said.

"Ah," said Vallora in a sympathetic tone, "politics. My condolences. My wife is in politics. Messy stuff."

Reed found himself hard pressed not to stare at Vallora in disbelief and indignation. *My wife is in politics. Messy stuff.* That was certainly *one* way to describe Empress Tansy Rose and her nine-century war to own the entire world. Reed could not decide if this was a joke, and if so, at whose expense.

The implications were lost on Gladys. She said, entirely serious, "Aye. Sometimes I go back to advise my successor. My second cousin, a spitfire young woman. Ain't an easy job, being bandit queen."

"I imagine not," said Vallora, "and you, Reed? I assume music is your trade, not just a hobby?"

Reed nodded. "You're right, but I am semi-retired, myself. Made a good bit of coin in my early years—nearly worked myself to death to meet public demand and popularity. Now I live a peaceful, frugal existence."

"Showbusiness can be brutal," Vallora agreed solemnly. "I love a good musical, been to quite a few over the years. But I heard from a friend that all that performing and traveling can be quite hard on the creative mind and body."

Reed wondered what lucky soul might count themselves among the Undying

Hero's *friends.* He hadn't supposed Vallora had any, not *real* friends, anyway. How could you trust that any of them were there for *you* as a person and not the fame and fortune of your title? Or worse, how could you be sure none of them were enemies in disguise?

Perhaps he was projecting, given their current mission.

Reed said, "I still play, obviously. You heard me in the bar. So long as I have breath in my lungs and blood in my heart, there'll be music comin' out my lips and fingers. Music is a language of the soul, you know."

Vallora's dark eyes crinkled at the corners. "You're a true artist, I can tell."

At that moment, Karsten arrived with their food, smiling warmly. The cheese was arranged on a wooden plate engraved to look like a clock—like the city itself. Every odd hour there was a different sample, three little bites speared through with toothpicks or smeared onto a little wooden spoon. Every even hour, there was a condiment or accompaniment of some kind.

"Everything you see here is made with

ingredients sourced from within Zenith," Karsten said, "specifically, from the very district indicated by its arrangement on the plate."

"I had no idea there was so much variety within the Circumference," Vallora said, eying the plate with interest.

Karsten chuckled. "Well, they say Zenith is a 'melting pot' of cultures, after all. The Empire has its fingers in a lot of pies... it should be of no surprise those flavors all end up here, in the Capital."

They started with the hour of one o'clock. The cheese was soft and white, lacking in scent save for that of fresh dairy. On the tongue, it was creamy and nearly flavorless—until mixed with a little All Purpose Marmalade from the two o'clock spot. It balanced the sweet and bitter jam perfectly.

"What you're tasting now is fresh goat's milk cream from satyr immigrants in Onest, paired with a classic All Purpose Marmalade from Twoil," Karsten explained as the trio considered the messages their tastebuds were sending.

Vallora raised an eyebrow and gave a little chuckle. "I have two questions," she said, holding up two fingers.

Karsten nodded for her to continue, curious to know what those questions would be. They knew who Vallora was, but was uncertain whether the Hero would reveal a nine-hundred-year-old knowledge of the city and its inhabitants... or ignorance thereof. Certainly the Official Narrative never presented Vallora as the *brightest* member of the Party, but Karsten doubted that someone with such a lifespan could go so long without picking up a thing or two.

"One," said Vallora, "*Where* do they keep goats in Onest? Isn't that more of a thing for Harvestrad?"

Harvestrad, the Fourth District, was where all the official farming and raising of livestock was done within the Circumference. More happened out on the Rim, but it was convenient to have food closer and more readily available in a city of this size, with so many mouths to feed. *Too many* mouths; most of what was produced in Harvestrad went to those living in the Middle and Inner Circumference, even though they were less populated than the Outer. There was not quite enough left over.

Karsten cleared their throat and said, politely, "Wherever they can. Communal gardens and such. Many of them are considered a part of the families they belong to. The milk production is an added bonus."

The satyrs looked a bit like goats themselves. From the waist up, they resembled humans; from the waist down, they had fur, digitigrade legs, and hooves. Some had horns, and all possessed those peculiar rectangular pupils in their eyes.

Other races might think it strange that they kept as pets and livestock creatures with such visible similarities to themselves, but to the satyrs, it made perfect sense. They and the goats were, after all, spiritual Cousins. Why would it be at all strange to keep your Cousins close by and well cared for?

Vallora's face brightened. "Oh, I see! Now, my second question is: what is in All Purpose Marmalade? It certainly isn't orange peels—at least not *just* orange peels."

"It's whatever fruit bits and peels—and sometimes vegetable—are left from your lunch pail at the end of the workday," Karsten explained. "There may be orange in there. There may be many other things besides. And quite a lot of sugar, of course."

"Thrifty," said Vallora, looking impressed.

Gladys and Reed were *not* impressed. What was 'thrifty' to Vallora was, to them, about survival. Each had spent time in Onest and Twoil, the first and second districts, where most new arrivals lived and worked upon immigrating to the Capital. The Outer Circumference was a crowded, troubled place. The middle class Middle Circumference and the high-class Inner Circumference were posher. People there were wary and standoffish, often abandoning the ways of their homelands for whatever the Zenith nobility was calling *culture* that day—lest they find themselves cast out and down like the rest.

They moved on to the hours of three and four o'clock. The cheese was firm, sharp, and had an overall pleasing, savory profile. It was the sort of thing you'd eat a great hunk of alongside a fresh loaf of crusty bread or, in this case, crackers. It wasn't so pungent that you tired of it fast, nor was it so bland that it couldn't stand on its own. The crackers were thin, with large bubbles, and well-salted.

"Now, here is your standard Zenith-style cow's milk cheese from Harvestrad," Karsten explained, "along with crackers baked in the sort of stone ovens that were engineered in Treon, after Zenith was moved from its original location. The change in altitude quite altered a lot of baking techniques, you know."

Vallora said wryly, "Not something they thought about while trying to save everyone from destruction by the Nightmare King, I bet."

"Aye, I imagine it wasn't highest on the Hero's list of priorities," said Reed.

He was grateful he had something to chew on so he wouldn't grind his teeth in frustration. According to the official stories, *Vallora* was the one who'd led the ancient ritual that tore the very land the Capital was built on from the planet and magically deposited it back on the ground somewhere else, away from the Nightmare King's explosive death throes.

Never mind that Vallora was probably the one who caused the Nightmare King to explode in the first place. The Official Narrative painted the enemy's death as a choice to self-destruct, but there were... other versions of that story. Ones which had nearly been stamped out by the Empire over the centuries, but which managed to survive through word of mouth.

Next came five and six o'clock. This was a cheese with bits in it. Spicy bits, little flecks of pepper which set the otherwise mild dairy product on fire. If this cheese was the right hook that sent you spinning, its accompaniment was the left hook that knocked you out of the ring: giant green olives stuffed with equally giant cloves of raw garlic.

"No need to explain this one," Vallora said to Karsten, stifling a burp. Gladys let hers out at maximum volume, and Reed shook his head and held up six fingers out of ten. She could do better. "It's the taste of the theater! Can't go to a venue in Hextory without running into dragon peppers and elephant garlic. Didn't know they were locally grown."

"Yes, mainly in Quintuoso, where the performers live," Karsten said.

Vallora looked to Reed with a hunger that had nothing to do with cheese. "You live in District Five, I expect? How is it? A riotous den of hedonism and creativity?"

"Well, you get used to the smell," said Reed. He jerked his thumb at Gladys. "Or else you have no sense of smell to begin with, like Gladdy."

Gladys, who didn't appear to have been bothered at all by the level of spice, grinned. "Smell's not the trouble. It's the performers who're always makin' a gods-damned *racket*, interrupting my sleep—"

"*What* sleep?" asked Reed.

"I get a good four hours," said Gladys. "Trained m'self back in my twenties to compress it all down so's less chance someone might get the better of me unawares. Bein' asleep is basically being unconscious."

"Yeah, and the way *you* sleep, you're basically *dead*."

This was a joke they rehashed often, but in truth, there had been a few times where Reed was *certain* that his best friend, who was Getting Old for a human, had actually kicked the bucket. He'd lost his otherwise impenetrable cool over Gladys's extraordinarily still body, which seemed not even to breathe when she was deep in slumber. Singing, screaming, brass horns, and the like failed to wake her, contrary to her complaint about the neighborhood. Only the glint of moonlight on a sharp blade or the retort of a Watch musket could bring Gladys back to reality.

Vallora asked, in a curious tone of voice, "Are you two roommates?"

Gladys nodded, and Reed said, "For the last fifteen years, give or take."

Vallora's curious tone deepened. "Are you… a couple?"

"No," they replied in tandem. They glared at one another, which made Vallora laugh.

"Sorry," said Vallora, looking appropriately contrite. "I just wanted to be sure I wasn't missing something."

"Ain't nothin' to be missed," said Gladys. "I never did care about none o' that stuff. *Romance.* Tried sex once just to see and didn't think much of it. Got m'son Gary for the trouble."

Reed shrugged and said, "I've never been interested, either. I met Gladys while doing some, well, charity work, wherein she needed a place to stay. For some reason she's never left. Can't understand why."

"From what *I* understand, *you're* the one who won't leave *her*, Reed," said Karsten with a sly grin.

Reed had a reputation for being the sort who could never walk past a beggar without handing over the contents of his wallet, never leave a stray litter of kittens out in the rain... never leave an older human woman to cope with what the Wars did to her son alone. He looked calm and collected on the outside, but on the inside, Reed was a molten forge of rage.

That rage had to go somewhere. Karsten wondered if Vallora would, in time, be on the receiving end of it. Reed might be angry, but he was also patient. He *waited.* That was why he was one of the senior officers for the Zenith chapter of the resistance. Fighting the Empire, in all its nine centuries of power, was nothing if not a waiting game.

Karsten smiled. "Let's move on to the next pairing, shall we? A nondairy nut cheese from trees that line the streets of Tyoctoon, with pickled mushrooms alongside, in the style of those sold in the

Septique Marketplace. Can you guess what sort of nut it's made with? I'll give you a hint: it's on the Merchant's Guild's official seal."

"That one is easy," said Vallora, smiling back. "It's acorns again."

# 6

## Literally Underground Theater

Things *might* have been all right if Andromeda hadn't stopped to talk to Tansy. Without that delay, she *might* have caught Vallora, Gladys, and Reed as they left Ale's Well That Ends Well. It would have saved her quite a lot of trouble, in addition to stopping this entire story in its tracks. But that is not the way that stories *go*—even those approved of by the Guild of Narrative in the Empire, known colloquially as GONE.

The way that stories go is that 'good' and 'bad' timing are a matter of what best benefits the audience rather than its players. Andromeda tended to see herself as the former rather than the latter, unaware that when she accepted the position of Vallora's bodyguard thirty years ago, she had made a Choice that would dictate the way the rest of her entire life played out.

Hers, and everybody else's in the Empire.

Because of the delay with Tansy, Andromeda stood outside of Ale's Well That Ends Well around the same time that the unlikely trio was finishing up their clock-based cheese plate. So it was that she remained just far enough behind them to let the story go on with itself.

Destiny sat beside her, sniffing the ground. Vallora had definitely been here, but her scent had changed dramatically. Destiny wondered what in the seven hells her best friend had been eating and why *she* hadn't been there to try some. Vallora always shared food with the Dog. That was how they originally became friends in those hazy days of yore.

Maybe she could get someone *else* within the pub to give her the same food Vallora had eaten. Andromeda had stopped just long enough to grab them each a roast turkey leg for a late lunch, but Destiny was *always* hungry.

Andromeda, for her part, was feeling queasy. She surveyed the exterior of Ale's Well That Ends Well from its crumbling brick walls to the chipped glass windows, which failed to contain the raucous noise levels within. She did not like crowds. She did not like noise. Or too many smells.

Joining the Watch when she was young had given her some control over those things—namely, the ability to disperse those *causing* the crowd, noise, and smells—and the Royal Guard had even more power over such matters. However, there were Rules. Nothing that had been written down, nothing you'd find in the official Code of Conduct or the Zenith lawbooks. They were unspoken rules of society and class, which when broken led to deeply uncomfortable and even dangerous situations.

Andromeda, who had difficulty reading between the lines or hearing what was *not* being said, had learned these rules the hard way.

Here it was: a single uniformed Royal Guard could not simply walk into a Lower Circumference bar on her own. A trio of Guards might have been all right, especially if they were off duty and in plainclothes. But the uniform meant Business. It screamed *I have authority over you and I intend to use it.* The trouble was that it was difficult to use one's legal authority when outnumbered thirty to one. Without companions, she would have a big, metaphorical target painted on her back.

Well, she'd just have to have to change. This was Hextory, after all. It didn't take long to find a shop selling stage costumes, though it did take a bit to find one made from a fabric that her sensitive skin could agree with. It was a cotton peasant dress with a square neckline and long sleeves. The mustard color and fanciful red embroidery was not her favorite nor a good match for her pale skin and hair, but it would do.

She found the closest Watch station, where she changed and stashed her armor and other garments in a locker. The officers on duty didn't question her. They were used to ditching their uniforms and heading out to a play or two between shifts.

Once more standing before the pub, feeling strange in her new dress, Andromeda shook her hands and cracked her knuckles nervously. Then she went inside, followed closely by Destiny.

The pub was full to bursting now. There were all sorts of creatives seated around the tables and clustered at the bar, dressed in bright colors and costume jewelry. They argued vehemently about truth and beauty, about politics and death, and gossiped about anyone in their social circle who had the poor luck not to be in the room. They were cutthroat and ragtag and lowbrow—and proud of it.

They were waiting for the show to begin. One that broke every rule set by GONE, though of course it had never been submitted for approval in the first place. This script was written in dark corners under new moons, kept carefully between the folds of yesterday's newspaper and rehearsed in back rooms with good soundproofing.

Behind the bar, Gary was selling beers that doubled as theater tickets. There was a non-alcoholic option, too, but it wasn't terribly popular among his clientèle: poor and half-starving actors, musicians, painters, novelists, poets, and playwrights. They tended to want to get at least a *little* drunk at their illegal dinner theater.

Andromeda did not want to get drunk. She stood by the bar for a good fifteen minutes before she was able to catch Gary's attention, then ordered the sparkling apple juice. Destiny was by now skulking under tables for scraps and begging from the other customers, so clearly she didn't need Andromeda to order for her.

Gary, none the wiser as to her Royal Guard identity, gave her a curt nod, then jerked his head towards the tiny corner stage. "On the left, then," he said. He tapped the side of his nose meaningfully. If asked exactly *what* was on the left, he would say it was the restroom. People rarely asked.

Andromeda just stared at him. It was all very well she didn't crane her head around, looking as lost as she felt, which might have aroused suspicion. She'd just been about to ask if someone fitting Vallora's description had come through here, but

Gary's strange words and gestures threw her off track. Her brow furrowed as she analyzed what they could *possibly* mean. Her mind was a branching fractal tree of possibilities.

Beside her, a stout halfling ordered a beer ticket. She saw the thoughts whirling across Andromeda's face and chuckled.

"First timer, eh? Come on, I'll show ya the ropes," said the halfling, and gestured for Andromeda to follow.

*This is not what I'm here for*, Andromeda thought, but she trotted obediently behind the halfling anyway. She had been a guard for over a century now. Obedience was in her bones, regardless of the rank she now carried.

Besides, she was curious. She gave a sharp whistle and Destiny appeared at her knee, gnawing on something unidentifiable.

Cleverly disguised beneath the corner stage was a set of stairs. They led to an underground hallway, off which there was a dingy basement storeroom and the actual bathroom, judging by the smell. The hallway ended in what looked like a wooden slat wall.

The halfling knocked on the 'wall' and one of the slats slid open, revealing a pair of suspicious eyes. The halfling raised her drink with the label clearly visible. The eyes blinked, then looked to Andromeda. They took in her sparkling apple juice and blinked again.

"Does the dog have a ticket?" asked a voice which presumably belonged to the same body as the eyes.

Andromeda glanced at Destiny, who wagged her tail and woofed softly. She dropped what she had been chewing on, which turned out to be a label from the same kind of beer the halfling was holding.

"Looks like it does," said the halfling, amused. "Would you look at *that*."

The 'wall' slid open.

Beyond was a much larger room than Andromeda was expecting, not that she had any expectations in the matter. It was again a good thing that she wasn't an outwardly expressive person, or else her shock might have drawn unwanted attention. As it were, she simply clutched her bottle hard and *stared*.

It was a theater. That much was clear. Someone had dug the hard-packed earth into a bowl shape, with seats placed in rows all along. They were not matching seats but clearly picked off from rubbish heaps and close-out sales, lovingly repaired and arranged into a thoughtful enough pattern. The seats were about three-quarters full, their occupants whispering gaily amongst themselves. There was a distinct air of anticipation and mischief about.

At the bottom of the bowl was the stage. It, too, had been carefully crafted from castoff materials, giving it the same look as a well-loved paperback book. The patched velvet curtains were an overcooked pea green color that Andromeda found extremely distasteful. Likely it was purchased at a steep discount because she couldn't imagine anyone actually *wanting* it.

Her halfling guide waved to a small group near the front, who waved back with a quiet cheer. Destiny trotted in to join them and received many soft coos and pets before settling herself into a seat. Andromeda hung back at the end of the row while they looked at her curiously, but the halfling gestured for her to join, so she did.

"Found a couple of new friends at the bar," said the halfling. "Our numbers grow."

One of her friends, a dwarf with her beard dyed pink, snorted. "Sounds so ominous when you put it like that.

"Well, shouldn't it be?" said another halfling with a devious smirk. "What's the fun of belonging to an underground secret theater society if you can't have a little fun with it?"

Andromeda had already worked this out, but there it was, right out in the open: this was a Backstage. She had stumbled into an actual, real, live Backstage, and was about to witness a very unsanctioned, absolutely illegal, borderline blasphemous *play*. Presumably by *unregistered actors*.

This was abhorrent, appalling, absolutely *heinous*, and it was also amazing. It was thrilling. She didn't have time for this with Vallora still on the lam, but she also couldn't *not* make time for this. Not just because it was her duty to figure out who these people were and report them to the proper authorities, but because *Andromeda loved theater*.

Once the others stopped chuckling, she cleared her throat and said, "We didn't get a playbill?"

"'Course not," said the pink-bearded dwarf. "Can you imagine? That'd be like, hundreds of little pieces of evidence floating around for the Watch or GONE to find, wouldn't it?"

"Oh. That makes sense," said Andromeda.

She was a bit crushed. Not, she told herself, because she wanted to add it to her organized collection of playbills from every show she'd ever seen, but because that *would* have made reporting them so much easier. She shouldn't have underestimated their wiliness in that respect.

Her halfling guide patted the chair arm between them and smiled. "Don't worry lass, you go to enough of these shows, you get to know the performers. Well, you get to know their *dramatis persona,* but that's enough in these dark halls."

Andromeda nodded. She had to blend in, pretend she was one of them. Doing so was not one of her strengths, but she would extend the effort for such a rare and important situation as this.

The lanterns lining the room flickered blue. It was some sort of spell flame, the sconces inscribed with runes she couldn't make out in the gloom. A hush fell over the crowd, and all eyes turned toward the front. The lanterns dimmed to near darkness. The show was about to begin.

The ugly green curtains parted, revealing a beautifully painted set made to look like a cottage on the edge of the woods, with farmland stretching out in the distance. The false chimney even puffed occasional gouts of steam into the air. Andromeda's eyes widened and she leaned forward in her seat, taking it all in. She wished she could take notes without worrying that would be against the rules of secrecy. The little bound book she kept in her pocket at all times was filled with messy shorthand done in dark rooms while staring at brightly lit stages.

"Once upon a time," boomed an unseen voice, "before the laws of nature were upended by the might of Empire, when death still meant actually *dying*, there lived in a house on the Rim two middle-aged farmers of no particular significance."

Andromeda frowned. That was *not* how

the classic opening lines went. 'Once upon a time,' yes, but not what followed it. The laws of nature upended? When death still meant actually dying? What did that even mean? They were accusations against the Empire, surely, but of *what*?

As for the 'two middle-aged farmers of no particular significance,' they couldn't be who she thought they were. There was no way. No matter how familiar the setup looked, that wouldn't make sense, because Father and Mother Leontyne were two of the most significant characters to ever live. They were also elderly, not middle-aged. She'd seen *The Origin of the Hero* dozens of times, so she would know. The actors playing Vallora's foster parents *always* had wrinkles and snow-white hair.

Then again, this *was* a play written, directed, and performed by heretics. Andromeda's frown deepened.

Two human actors emerged from the cottage, bickering about minute farmhouse chores, clearly exasperated in that way couples could be when they'd been together a long time but never really bothered to listen. They were wearing simple homespun clothes, and the masculine one had a pitchfork in hand. They were wearing wigs and their faces were so heavily painted with stage makeup that they were effectively anonymous.

Andromeda could see the contouring that had been used to change the visual shape of their faces, something she'd learned about when Vallora had gotten them backstage access to talk to the Royal Theatre Company. It was annoyingly well done. They might as well be new people entirely.

The players strolled along the stage until they reached the painted backdrop of trees, beneath which there lay a large woven basket with a lid. They stood on either side of it as the argument grew ever more heated and absurd. Andromeda recognized the undercurrent of innuendo that was making the audience chuckle and awkwardly forced herself to laugh along with them. The sound rang out like a duck's quack across a pond.

*Great Mother Tree*, she thought, *you CANNOT have the Hero's foster parents make jokes about using FARM IMPLEMENTS like that! It's just not RIGHT!*

Suddenly the basket gave a wail that was, for one, not a baby's but a grown man's voice, and two, clearly coming from backstage. The latter was forgivable, but the former was an affront to common decency and respect, given that the baby was obviously meant to be Vallora. The crowd absolutely lost it laughing. Andromeda saw her halfling companion glance her way, trying to share in the amusement, and pretended to join them. Her forced expression would be harder to recognize in the dark.

"Well *shit*," said Father Leontyne, "is that a *baby*?"

Mother Leontyne bent over, waggling her rear end in a way that was supposed to be either comical or seductive, Andromeda couldn't tell which, and plucked a baby doll from the basket.

"It *is* a baby! Just what we needed to solve all our marital problems!" she exclaimed.

The audience lost it again. Andromeda laughed for real this time, but out of anger, not amusement. This was a farce. An absolute farce. To think that someone had taken one of the most foundational stories of the Empire—a Story with a capital S if there ever was one—and turned it into a situational comedy was unthinkable.

It was also brilliant.

Andromeda had to hand it to the rebels; they were *good.* The dialogue was snappy, lines delivered loud and clear, the comedic timing was to the second, and the sets had clearly taken quite a lot of time and effort. The tension was strung like a well-tuned lute, and the message of the story built in such a way that you couldn't poke a single hole in its logic, though it might be the logic of heresy.

In the original tale, baby Vallora, still mortal, was found abandoned in a basket by an elderly human couple who never had children due to infertility. Mother Leontyne was sweet and doting while Father Leontyne was stoic and gruff, but with a good heart. They were perfect soul mates, exactly as you'd expect. Not this bumbling, arguing, couple with problems and half a dozen kids of their own, all of whom were put to work in the fields.

In the original, they raised Vallora to be a strapping young farm boy, a cheerful, helpful lad despite the fact that he wasn't quite accepted by the community. The usual tale never said exactly *why* Vallora was an outcast, and Andromeda had never thought to question it. *This* version said it was because Vallora soon revealed herself to be, well, a *her* rather than a *him*, and people in Meridian back then didn't like that sort of thing.

Andromeda didn't know if this was *true* (Vallora herself never spoke about this part of her life), but at the very least it was more compelling. Given Andromeda's personal experience with local sexism, probably more realistic, too. Perhaps the heretic writers had done that *one* detail better, at least.

The original story saw Vallora winning over the community by rescuing Princess Tansy from the clutches of a fierce young dragon whose hoard was in the mountains above Vallora's little community. Andromeda had seen a full range of attempts to portray Hanzelfrost, the Butcher of Mount Savor, from cutouts to puppets to multi-actor costumes with pyrotechnics. Certainly some were better than others—her favorite was the crystal-powered animatronic employed by the

Royal Theatre Company, who had the budget for such things. It sparkled and glittered and the gouts of flame it shot were *amazing*.

There was no dragon in this story. Instead, Tansy (who was portrayed with *the most* unflattering makeup possible, her droopy eyes always leaking) was held hostage by the local baron and his men after a visit to negotiate land tithes went awry. He had the same name as the dragon, but with a space inserted in the middle. Baron Hanzel Frost, the Butcher of Mount Savor.

How *dare* they make an exciting magical conflict into a political one? But that's what you got with rebels, she supposed. They were all about politics.

In the story she knew, Vallora left with Tansy after being told about the threat of the Nightmare King, believing that she could save the Empire as a whole. In this one, Vallora left because, by rescuing Tansy from the Baron, she'd sided with the monarchy and lost the trust of the common folk who just wanted to be free from tyranny. If she'd stayed, they surely would have hunted her down with torches and pitchforks.

Quite a statement to make. Andromeda had never seen or read a story with an unhappy ending before. It unsettled and fascinated her at the same time.

*If this is what their propaganda looks like, no wonder they've been impossible to remove from the Empire,* Andromeda thought as the actors took their final bow. *It's convincing. It's entertaining. They know what it is they're doing.*

That made them all the more a threat, and she shivered as the audience applauded silently, hands raised and fingers waving, the same way applause was given by the Deaf and hard of hearing. Andromeda thought that if they'd *actually* cheered, the roar would be so great that the Watch would be called in for a noise violation, and it would all be over.

"Got the good goosebumps, eh?" asked her halfling seatmate, elbowing Andromeda in the ribs. "How'd you like your first show?"

Andromeda collected her thoughts from where they lay scattered in chaos on the floor of her mind.

"It was... enlightening. I rather think

I've been inspired to… tell a few friends about it," she said.

The halfling clapped her on the shoulder. "Good! Welcome to the resistance!"

# 7

## Deep Fried Plans (on a Stick)

As evening approached, Vallora, Gladys, and Reed made their way toward Nonigate, where commercial airships arrived with goods from all across the Empire. There weren't many restaurants, but there *were* untold numbers of street vendors selling food to the dock workers, much of it in a form you could eat with one hand.

As such, food in Nonigate either came on a stick or inside of a hand pie. There was no limit to what the clever vendors managed to shove into these formats, laws of physics and cooking be damned. Given that this was the city's airport, it was possible to get your hands on just about any ingredient you could imagine from around the world and then some.

It was easy to put anything you wanted into a hand pie, given it was basically an edible envelope. Lately the trend was to create "The Unending Empire in One Bite," which meant pies filled with chicken from the Capital, rice noodles from Luster, hot pepper from Tang, apricot jam from Piquant, pickled green tomatoes from Verve, brined sheep's cheese from Revel, and so on, all inside a single crust. Every bite was an explosion of flavors; whether those flavors actually melded together was often ignored. It was the novelty of the thing that mattered.

Food served on a stick was much the same: an attempted multi-course meal on a single wooden skewer. At least with these, a person could eat one bite at a time... so long as the skewer was well-constructed and the removal of a load-bearing banana did not cause the entire thing to slide off onto the cobblestones below. Some enterprising chef had discovered that if a food couldn't be skewered in its original state, battering and deep frying it would solve the problem, and so the technology spread.

Which is how Vallora came to be eating buttered lemonade—on a stick. Lemonade was a sweet and sour drink from down around the Aromal Sea. The addition of butter, which the vendor said her grandmother made by small batch in the old Relish style, would have made residents of the Aromal Sea curse the heavens in bewildered outrage, but was surprisingly good. The flavor was sweet and sour and salty and *rich.*

"Don't see how y'can fry a *drink*," Gladys said, eyeing her stick with suspicion. Vallora had insisted on treating the three of them, claiming that food tasted better in good company.

"The chef said she freezes it into ice cubes first, then wraps it in dough," explained Vallora. "It's only in the fryer for a moment, and in that time—"

She took a bite from the stick. Beneath the crispy brown outer layer of fried dough and powdered sugar oozed a sweet, tangy substance which coated the tongue and throat like sunshine dribbling through an overgrown alley on a still summer morning.

Reed swallowed his first bite, surprised by how much he enjoyed it. "Haven't seen *ice cubes* in a very long time. Not even in a drink, much less a deep fryer."

Vallora chewed thoughtfully. "No? I thought everyone had a refrigerator these days."

"A re-fricking-what?" said Gladys.

"It's a fancy crystal-powered box that keeps things cold," Reed explained. "Rich folk use them to keep food from going bad. And to make ice."

"Rich folk?" repeated Vallora. "The new technology was supposed to be available for everyone, at every class level. That's what the Merchant and Shipping Guilds said would happen if they were allowed to hold individual patents. The competition would drive the price down."

Gladys let out a loud, "Hah!" and ate the rest of her fried buttered lemonade in one go, cheeks bulging with dough and amusement.

"You seem to know quite a bit about it," said Reed casually. "You in one of the guilds?"

Vallora's gaze slid away. "I've worked with them."

The three of them wandered through Nonigate at a leisurely pace. It was not the sort of place for a stroll, having been constructed to move crates and sacks and barrels and various vehicles rather than pedestrians. Boxy warehouses lined the wide streets in various states of upkeep, some pristine stone monoliths that spoke of noble backing, others ramshackle hodgepodges of wood and tin sheeting. Crystal-powered smallships maneuvered through the streets with solar sails drawn tight, undersides hovering just above the piles of dung which were the natural consequence of the older horse-drawn carts still in use by poorer merchants.

"Have either of you done much traveling outside the Capital?" Vallora asked, doing a sidestep around a particularly fresh pile of grassy poo.

"I've been on tour a bit," said Reed, patting his lute case.

"I was born in the Hundred Mile Waste," Gladys said. "By the time I were twenty I knew it like the back of my own hand.

Made m'way past the borders into Verve and Relish and Gravy… made it as far as Tang, once, by accident."

Tang was on the other side of the globe, a paradisaical valley surrounded by imposing mountains and caves of unfathomable terrors. Vallora had fought some of them in the deepest darks, defeating the ancient secret society which had for centuries prevented travelers and traders from entering the valley. Afterward, Tang had been put under eternal protection of the Empire, and the Empire got access to the pungent spices that grew there.

It was a win-win situation, repeated hundreds of times across the world they all shared. The motto of the Empire was, after all: *Stronger United, Stronger as One.*

Some people disagreed.

"By accident? Really," said Vallora, fascinated. "How did that happen?"

Gladys tossed her skewer over her shoulder; it landed point-down right in the center of the pile of poop. Reed watched Vallora's eyes follow it, taking note. Gladys's preferred weapon was the chipped morning star that hung on her hip (its name was *Skull Cracker*), but she was also adept at throwing knives and many other things besides. They didn't call her The Destroyer for nothing.

"Hid from the Authorities in a pickle barrel. Pickle barrel got put on an airship. Airship went to Tang," Gladys explained simply.

"Did you spend the entire time in the barrel?" Vallora asked, knowing a royal flight to Tang took two days without stopping.

"Why not? Food and drink was all right there. Never have gotten rid o' the smell, though."

Gladys pushed back her sleeve and held her pale, wrinkly arm out for Vallora to sniff. Vallora did so without a moment's hesitation. Reed wasn't sure if this was impressive or just plain foolish. Maybe after nine-hundred years, you simply stopped giving a shit.

"Spiced cauliflower pickles!" Vallora exclaimed, and Gladys nodded smugly.

It was at this moment that, many streets away, Andromeda finally emerged from the Backstage theater and managed to get it out of Old Kurt that Vallora *had* been in the pub, and was ultimately headed for Nonigate. Had mentioned something about a world food tour and a friend with an airship.

Gladys did not know this, but she did know *something* relevant had happened; the smug look fell from her face, her sinews pulled taught, and she stood up ramrod straight. One hand smacked her leg with the baton piece in it.

"Someone's after us," she said, scowling. "I can feel it."

"Oh, I'm sure they've been after us all day," Vallora said calmly. "I'd best get a move on. You're both welcome to come, if you like. Not an adventure without companions by your side. Might get a bit dangerous, though. I have a habit of running into trouble."

*I'll bet you do*, Reed thought, *and you don't mean with the Watch or the Royal Guard. You mean Story Trouble. Protagonist Trouble. World-shattering stakes Trouble. And only someone as strong as the Undying Hero would risk trusting two obviously shady old strangers she just met in a bar.*

Reed adjusted the lute case on his back.

He always carried an extra set of clothes and a couple pairs of underwear in it for emergencies. There was also a tattered songbook, a flask, and a bottle of arthritis pills for Gladys, who refused to take any sort of medication unless Reed threatened her with sappy love songs.

That would have to be enough for now. He had more things stashed away in the City of Whispers, where, if things went according to plan, the three of them would eventually end up. Since leaving his old life behind, he'd made do with less. Gladys certainly had as well.

Reed lifted his cap to Vallora and did a little bow. "Be happy to come along! It's been a while since I picked up some new songs from other lands."

"I'm bored," Gladys added, "so all right. You gonna pay our way?"

"You won't need to spend a single copper," Vallora assured her. "Now, help me find an airship called *My Daring Darling*, and we'll make sure Captain St—whoever is following us doesn't catch up."

# 8

## Cat's Got Your Tongue

*My Daring Darling* was a Shard Speeder. That much was apparent from its sleek almond hull and seven aft-tilted sails. Her crystal core was a jagged slice of obsidian, temperamental, with knife's-edge acceleration, which made her faster than anything else in the skies. The ship was also many shades of pink, from deep magenta to neon to the palest blush. Her name was painted on the nose in flashy, curling script made to look like ribbons.

Shard Speeders were usually pleasurecraft, not cargo carriers, but this one was being loaded with *something* in heavily guarded metal crates. The guards were not City Watch, but the personal mercenaries of a noble house, given the elaborate silver crests on their armor. Not law enforcement, per se, but that didn't mean they wouldn't turn someone like Vallora, Reed, or Gladys over to the authorities if a reward were involved.

Most of the guards were panthera, a bipedal race who looked like humans crossed with common housecats. Their long tails swished and curled purposefully as they checked and double-checked their cargo, projecting an air of competence and ease.

"What's the plan?" Reed asked from their position behind a row of abandoned crates. "Are these friends of yours?"

"The captain is," Vallora replied, "or rather, she will be."

"We talkin' intimidation, or blackmail?" Gladys asked.

"Oh, nothing like that," said Vallora. "I've known her family for a very, *very* long time, but the two of us have never met."

"Does she even know you're coming?" asked Reed, hoping that 'never met' meant in person, and that they still might have exchanged letters or crystal communications.

Vallora grinned cheerfully and walked back toward the vendor area. “Nope! Come on, then, I’ve figured out a plan. We’re going to take a leaf out of Ms. The Destroyer’s book.”

“I don’t own no books,” Gladys said proudly, “on account of I don’t know how'ta *read*.”

Reed watched Vallora reconsider her words. “We’re going to take inspiration from your daring past exploits with the pickles,” she said, “and get food involved.”

***

The trio returned to *My Daring Darling’s* docking bay with heavily laden cart, wearing the cleanest linen aprons they could find. Vallora had a white chef’s hat which fitted awkwardly over her chunky hair twists; Reed was amazed but unsurprised that it made the Hero look charming rather than absurd. Maybe Vallora’s incredible charisma was the *real* power she carried within.

There were no more crates waiting to be loaded, and much of the guard had either left or boarded the ship. Two panthera stood beside the loading platform, going over their checklists one final time. Both were wearing leather armor with blue surcoats, the coat-of-arms on which featured a tiger with a two-headed snake in its mouth.

The tiger was wearing a bow around its neck. Both of the guards looked bored.

"Hullo there! Looks like we made it just in time," Vallora called as they approached.

The two panthera turned and eyed them suspiciously, tails curling into question marks. Both were toms barely out of their adolescent kitten years. One was a rakishly scruffy tabby, the other a sleek ginger.

"Pardon?" said the Ginger, big green eyes darting between the trio and his clipboard in confusion.

"Who're you?" the Tabby asked with a growl. He puffed out his chest.

"The caterers!" Vallora exclaimed, gesturing at the cart. "A last minute addition, surprise gift from the Captain's mothers."

The strong scent rising off of the hand pies and skewers was nearly visible to the naked eye. The nostrils flared on both panthera, their sense of smell forty times that of humans, elves, or halflings. The Ginger licked his lips with a pink tongue, but the Tabby shot him a warning look.

"All three of you?" he asked, gesturing at Reed and Gladys.

Reed was unassuming enough, but Gladys clearly came from a life of battle and conflict. Everything she wore was leather or fur and had too many straps. Her skin was scarred and her face hardened, her expression lacking even a single drop of the deference for customers that the service industry required.

"Master Reed here is also the in-flight entertainment," Vallora said, gesturing to the lute case on Reed's back. She leaned in over the cart, and both toms leaned in, too. Vallora's voice dropped to a stage whisper. "I know how she looks, but Mistress Gladys is actually a survivor of the Fifty-Seventh Street Molasses Incident."

Gladys put on a solemn face. "It all cooked into candy, you know, the molasses, because of the heat from the explosions. The doctors had to cut it all off—along with skin and hair and—"

"Ah, yes, I see," the Tabby said, stopping her before she could get too graphic. "Still, we'll have to search you and your wares for contraband before you're let on."

They'd expected this. As a result, all of their weapons were skillfully hidden. Vallora's sword was rolled up in a fancy tablecloth filled with skewers. Reed's dirk was in a special compartment beneath his lute, wrapped in underwear. *Skull Cracker,* Gladys's morning star, had cut fruit stuck to all of the points in an artful fashion, disguising it as an edible centerpiece. Her throwing knives were, she promised, 'in places no one could get to without a full strip search,' which they had all agreed was unlikely.

While the panthera pawed at the cart, Vallora picked up a skewer and waved it about enticingly. The guards didn't look at it, but their ears did swivel in Vallora's direction. Reed could see their whiskers twitching.

"You know, it's a shame nobles never finish everything they order, when it comes to food," Vallora said.

The Ginger rolled his eyes. "I know! At least House Silverclaw donates their leftovers, though, 'tis a bit insulting, if you really think about it. Living off someone else's leftovers."

"Truly, it is!" Vallora agreed. "I bet they wouldn't notice if we arrived with a couple less cheese-and-herring-sandwiches-on-a-stick..."

The Tabby, who had been peering at the underside of the cart, straightened up. "Is that a bribe?"

"Do you want it to be?" Gladys asked. Reed barely refrained from kicking her in the shins. It only ever hurt his foot to do so, anyway. He ought to invest in a pair of steel-toed boots. Maybe Vallora would buy him some. She sure had dropped a huge amount of coin on the cart, food, and aprons already.

The Tabby narrowed his eyes at her, but his ears didn't flatten. He reached out and took the skewer from Vallora, claws flexed to show their sharp, curved points.

"My Mams always made us finish every scrap on our plates," he said. "Be a shame to let any extra go to waste."

Vallora handed the Ginger a skewer, then gave each of them a cherry balsamic hand pie as well. The guards munched on their spoils and waved the trio on up the loading dock. As they went, Reed heard the Ginger say,

"Told you 'twas a good luck to get assigned to Captain Jinny's ship."

"Aye. The Countesses spoil her rotten because she's an only child," responded the Tabby. "That's how come she got this ship last year, as an eighteenth birthday gift."

"Y'know, *I'm* eighteen... and I hear she's not opposed to dating below her station..."

The Tabby laughed. "Aye! So long as you don't mind coming second in her affections, after her love for this ship!"

"Why *would* I mind? Have you *seen* her?"

As the dock pulled up and the magnetic doors slowly locked into place, a third voice cut in, sharp and stern:

"Attention, soldiers of the House of Silverclaw! Have either of you seen Emperor Vallora the Undying Hero near here?"

If Tansy knew this was how Andromeda was 'discreetly' tracking down Vallora, she might have gone into a dead faint. But she did not know, and would not until later; by then the situation would be so out of hand that fainting was not an option. She would have *unpleasant work* to do, thanks to Andromeda's lack of tact.

"Y'know," said the Ginger thoughtfully, "I thought the big one looked familiar… I just figured there was no way it was possible that was actually *her*… not in *this* part of town…"

A dog barked. A large one, from the sound of it. One of the panthera hissed.

Vallora, already halfway down the hall, stopped and looked back, grinning. "Ooh, good work, Captain," she said, then added to Gladys and Reed, "Captain Stagge of the Royal Guard, not the Captain of this ship," as if they needed the clarification. Gladys's leg was smarting intensely.

With that, Vallora zoomed down the narrow walkway between crates, peering through round metal doorways until she found the galley. The cargo doors locked fully, and the rest of the conversation outside was cut off.

"Hm," said Reed.

"Is it just me," said Gladys, "or did she sound *happy* about the Authorities catchin' up with us?"

"I wonder," said Reed. "Well, things are about to get interesting. Let's go. I want to see *Val* make friends with *Captain Jinny*, whoever *she* is."

# 9

## Thirty-Sixth

After leaving the cart with the ship's cook, Vallora marched straight to the airship's bridge, cloak swooshing dramatically. It kept catching Reed in the face, and Gladys stepped on its edge once, though that didn't stop Vallora. The fabric tore like paper in the exact shape of Gladys's sole; Reed picked it up and tucked it into his pocket, in case it could be sold as a relic or used in a magic ritual of some kind later on.

Like the ship itself, the bridge was oval in shape, the far wall made entirely of thick crystal windows. The dashboards were polished mahogany and silver, the steering wheel carved to look like a wreath with a wooden bow on each spoke. The seats—there was a line of them facing the windows—were plush pink velvet with silver buttons. Everything looked more-or-less brand new.

Leaning on the steering wheel was a lovely female panthera with long midnight fur and piercing yellow eyes. She was wearing the crew uniform: deep blue jacket, slacks, and polished black boots. Her uniform had silver epaulets and a star pin on the collar, an obvious sign of rank.

Vallora stopped in the middle of the room, hands on hips. "Captain Silverclaw?"

The panthera woman tilted her head. If she was worried about the arrival of three strangers on the bridge, she didn't show it. "No. I'm only the First Mate, Sabah. The Captain's right behind you, though," she said, pointing over their shoulders.

The trio turned around.

Captain Jindra Beryl Sa'dina Silverclaw the 36th was nineteen years old, tiny, and absolutely thrilled to find Emperor Vallora the Undying Hero standing on the bridge of her airship. Her blue eyes, wide with excitement, took up half of her face. She was a calico, mostly white with aesthetically pleasing patches of tan, brown, and black. Notably, all three colors formed the shape of a heart in the center of her face.

Her large ears stood at attention, aimed directly at Vallora. Her mouth hung open, revealing a small pink tongue and long white canines. She pressed her paws together in front of her chest and made a happy sort of chirrup that stirred even Gladys's iron-cold heart.

Vallora said, "There you are! You look so much like your—what is it now? Thirty-somethingth great-grandmother?" She saluted smartly. "Congratulations on your captaincy! I'm sure your mothers are quite proud."

Jinny hopped from foot to foot. Her uniform had even more decoration than the others, all sorts of braided trim and embroidery and, if it wasn't obvious enough already, bows. The largest ribbon was clipped to the back of her head and stuck out on either side. The ends fluttered as she moved with excited feline grace.

"You're Emperor Vallora!" she yelled, in

a voice much louder than Reed or Gladys was expecting. "I recognize you from the paintings in the manor! Ohmygosh—is it finally time? Is it my turn to go on... an ADVENTURE?"

House Silverclaw was descended from one of the original Party members. Of those who embarked on the original quest to save the world from the Nightmare King, only Vallora, Tansy Rose, and the Dog had become immortal. The other three had become fabulously wealthy and powerful... and then died, but not before bearing heirs to their vast legacies.

Vallora spread her brawny arms wide, cloak billowing out behind her.

"It is! That is, if you'll have me? If you'll have—us?" she said, gesturing to Gladys and Reed. She flashed an apologetic smile at them. "No use pretending now."

"We knew who you were," Gladys said with a sniff.

"Oh, I know you did," Vallora replied. "How could you not? It was fun, acting otherwise. Almost felt like being a normal citizen, for once."

Somehow, this didn't come off as arrogant. Vallora's tone and happy-go-lucky expression were too genuine for that. Reed shook his head. Did that mean Vallora was pretending not to remember him? He thought of Captain Stagge and the Dog (the source of the barking could be no other) out in the docking bay and decided that was a question for later.

"We should get moving," Reed said.

Vallora snapped her fingers. "Right! Captain Jinny, I'm afraid the Royal Guard is on our tail," she said. "Can you get us out of here as fast as possible?"

Jinny saluted, her ribbons flaring. "Aye, right away, your Highness!"

"No need for titles, just call me Lora," Vallora replied, and Jinny chirruped in glee.

"Take a seat, friends, we're headed out!" Jinny shouted as she bounded up the the steering wheel.

First Mate Sabah gave a lazy salute, kissed the top of Jinny's head, and sauntered over to the navigation console. The fluid way she checked calculations, pulled levers, and pressed buttons showed a great deal of skill and experience, particularly in comparison to Jinny's overexcited mashing of the main controls.

Jinny pulled up a fancy crystal communicator set—the cryscom, as people had taken to calling the recent invention—and relayed instructions to the rest of the crew in a sing-song voice.

Vallora took the middle seat on the row of pink cushions; Reed sat to her right, and Gladys to the left. The ship's crystal core started with a rumble and the psychic scent of a hot cup of tea, the heat of a forge, and the sound of a steel knife being sharpened. Since no one but the highest ups knew how the magic that powered the Empire's airships worked, no one was certain why they induced phantom sensory information in their riders. Every ship's sensory effect was unique.

Reed realized he was seated beside the highest of all the higher-ups in the Empire and decided to ask about it.

Vallora gave him an apologetic smile and rubbed the back of her head. "Haven't the foggiest idea, to be honest. Every time the engineers tried to explain it to me, the fancy technical words they used went right over my head."

Reed found this answer suspicious, as did Gladys, who out of Vallora's sight rolled her eye and scowled.

As the ship made its way out of dock, in somewhat of a bumpy, start-and-stop fashion, Vallora continued, "Tansy says airship engines basically run on the same energy that souls do. I still don't know exactly what that means or how it's possible, but if she understands and accepts it, then it must be all right. Tans has always been very smart, and she cares about her people."

It was odd to hear someone refer to Undying Empress Tansy Rose, Healer of the World, as 'Tans.' Reed supposed it must sound odd to some folks when he called the fearsome Gladys the Destroyer 'Gladdy,' though. It was hard to think of Vallora as a person instead of The Hero, someone who didn't understand engineering jargon and made up cute nicknames for her loved ones, but he was already starting to.

Which was a dangerous thing, given the plans they had in mind.

The shipyard gates just ahead were still closed. Though the sky was open above them, a magical field prevented ships from coming or going except through sanctioned portals. Reed hadn't seen the huge, circular gates this close in a long time. They were eight stories tall, the copper facade green from weather. This side was etched with a stylized figure of the original Jindra Silverclaw, who appeared to be winking at him.

Jinny was speaking with Gate Control. They cleared her for departure, and the enormous gates were slowly sliding open when the cryscom crackled and whined ominously.

A new voice came on, saying: "Captain Silverclaw, this is Captain Andromeda Stagge of the Royal Guard speaking. You are to cease flight operations and re-dock your ship immediately."

Jinny looked to Vallora for instructions.

"Stall her until the gates are open," Vallora whispered, "then we'll leave!"

"Ooh, my first illegal activity," Jinny purred, "well, for this week."

"This week?" Reed and Gladys muttered at the same time. One of them was beginning to feel this was a dubious choice of ship, and the other was growing more enamored with the young captain.

Into the cryscom, Jinny said, in a

convincingly innocent voice, “Why?”

There was a pause on the other end. Everyone’s ears were on the cryscom, but their eyes were on the gates. They were, as many frustrated pilots had exclaimed in the foulest language possible, infuriatingly slow. Under the circumstances, the movement appeared infinitesimal.

“According to Code 423-A, I am not required to state the reason why,” Andromeda replied, sounding flustered. “You are to cease operations and dock now.”

Jinny did not need to be told how to play her part. “What’s Code 423-A? Is that in the Merchant Ship Code of Conduct, or the Royal Guard Code, or the Zenith Municipal Charter—”

She was cut off by the sound of Andromeda’s voice, definitely frustrated this time: “You do not need to know! This is a matter of royal security!”

“Oh really? Woooow,” said Jinny.

“Yes, really!” Andromeda said. Slightly reduced in volume, Andromeda, without taking her finger off the talk button, presumably turned to the Gate Control officer and demanded, “Why are the gates still opening? Close them!"

"I can't!" said Gate Control. "Do you know how these gates work? If you stop that kind of complicated machinery in the middle of operation at the wrong time, it could take weeks to get it going again!"

A convenient design flaw if there ever was one, thought Reed.

They heard Andromeda huff loudly. Her voice returned to full volume and she said into the cryscom, "Emperor Vallora Leontyne Rose, blessed be your name," (her intonation made it clear she intended the opposite of a blessing) "if you are on this ship—"

Vallora sprang up and gently took the cryscom from Jinny. "Hello, Captain! No need to worry! Just going for a little joyride! No kidnappers or ransomers or enemy agents involved, I promise!"

Reed and Gladys exchanged a glance. They'd been doing that so much today that Reed wondered if they were going to start exchanging thoughts next.

"Your Highness, I'm sorry, but you can't just," Andromeda struggled for words, "just go gallivanting off without—"

"Without saying goodbye in person? I'm

sorry, but you would have tried to talk me out of it, I'm afraid," Vallora interrupted, "and you can be very persuasive. Is Dez with you?"

The Dog barked, and the sound was clear enough that Andromeda must have held the receiver up to the canine's snout. A brilliant, if sad smile unfurled across Vallora's beautiful dark face.

She glanced through the front windshield. The gates were nearly wide enough for My Daring Darling to scrape through. Vallora gestured for Reed to join her by the wheel with Jinny, and to bring his lute. He did so, wondering what was about to happen.

"Sorry to you too, Dez! Be good for Captain Stagge, won't you?" Vallora said. "I'm afraid I'll be going now. Take care!"

"You—" said Andromeda.

Vallora held the receiver up to Reed. "What's the most annoying song in your repertoire?"

Reed struck up a chord heavy version of 'The Battle of Floret Field' and scream-sang the vocals into the receiver. The song was a damning indictment of the Empire's use of overwhelming military force, but given the delivery, it was difficult to tell unless you already knew the words.

Jinny bounced up and down beside him, punching the air with her fists. "YEAH! THAT'S THE STUFF!" Emboldened by her praise, Reed tossed his head back and upped the volume.

Despite this, they still heard Andromeda's growl of rage come through the cryscom. There was a clattering sound, followed by protests from Gate Control. The cabin was so tense that no one wondered who was still holding down the talk button through all of this. It was, in fact, the Dog, who seemed to think that what was going on in the Gate Control Tower was important for her Best Friend (Vallora) to know.

"Hey! Hey, Captain Stagge, ma'am, with all due respect, you can't just, do you even know how to fly one of those? Boarding gliders are only for serious emergencies, like a war—"

Andromeda's voice, faintly: "This is a serious emergency! As Emperor Vallora's bodyguard, I have authorization to use whatever means necessary to secure her safety and the safety of the Empire."

An engine started up.

"Oh dear," said Vallora, whose amused voice cut through the cacophony with ease. "Captain Jinny, I think we need to make a break for it."

# 10

## Battles and BFFs

Andromeda was not fooling around. She was *doing her job*. She was *not* going to let Vallora run headlong into danger in the company of potential rebels! The old man in the shady bar said Vallora left with two people: one a musician called Reed Thorley, and the other, if she was not mistaken, a human woman called *Gladys the Destroyer*. Not the sort of name that inspired trust. Plus, the pub where they'd met had a secret Backstage, which she assumed Reed and Gladys attended.

House Silverclaw wasn't trustworthy,

either. Andromeda lived and worked in the castle. She spent most of her day shadowing Vallora, including to political meetings. The Silverclaws might be Party descendants, but they had a reputation for being involved in smuggling rings and backing questionable forms of entertainment. For example, *why* would you build steam trains just to crash them together at full speed, risking the audience's lives in the ensuing explosion? It didn't make sense.

Andromeda hated nonsense. That's what this whole endeavor was. *Nonsense.*

She'd never set foot in a boarding glider, let alone piloted one, but the controls didn't look *too* different from the Royal Guard's hovercarts. The shallow, rectangular craft was made to pack a dozen soldiers and their weapons like sardines in a tin. Its main solar sail covered the open cabin like a tarp, and two more were deployed to each side, all marked with the Dawn Armada's rising sun insignia. Even while in its magnetic tether, the winds blowing in from the gates buffeted it around.

From what she could tell, a single pilot steered the craft while a gunner deployed the spiked grappling hook into the enemy ship's flank. They'd pull the craft up via the grappling hook cable, then storm the vessel and capture its helm. Andromeda would have to play all those roles herself.

She could do it. She hadn't become Captain of the Royal Guard for nothing.

Andromeda's stomach dropped as the glider rose, its little crystal core emanating the smell of fresh baked cinnamon rolls and the realization that you hadn't lost your glasses, they'd just been on top of your head the whole time. Andromeda didn't wear glasses, but she patted her head anyway. She found the magical sensations hard to escape, just like real world sensory input. *Sensitive,* her father always said, shaking his head, and she quashed the thought immediately.

*My Daring Darling* revved its engine.

Andromeda fired the grappling hook.

The projectile pierced the ship's outer hull just to the left of the main cabin door, its prongs springing open to hold it in place. Andromeda had two whole seconds to congratulate herself on the shot before *My Daring Darling* rocketed forward, clearing the gates at a very illegal speed and dragging the glider along with it.

It was almost fun.

There would be no pulling the glider alongside the ship at this speed. Andromeda instead increased her altitude, so that *My Daring Darling* was below her at an angle. Then she laid her short sword across the cable connecting the two ships and jumped.

That part was *definitely* fun.

Andromeda slid down the cable and thumped against the cabin door. She engaged the emergency release lever with her foot, then made a daring acrobatic leap inside, sword in hand.

Something heavy smashed into the panel beside her head and stuck fast. She glanced sideways and saw it was an iron morning star with, for some reason, a strawberry impaled on one of the spikes. Whoever had thrown it knew what they were doing. Whoever had thrown it was *strong*.

"One wrong move, and that'll be yer head next time," Gladys said, arm still outstretched.

Andromeda didn't answer. She used the precious seconds another person might have spent voicing a retort to take in the scope of the situation. Jinny, Vallora, and Reed at the helm, Sabah to her left, Gladys straight ahead. It was clear who her opponent was going to be, even though the wiry old woman was wearing a linen chef's apron over her leathers.

Andromeda dove forward and tucked herself into a roll. A knife whistled over her head.

"It's gonna be like that, is it?" said Gladys. "So be it."

When Andromeda popped up, Gladys was ready for her. Double daggers caught Andromeda's short sword and pushed back hard, forcing her into a defensive position. As indicated by the morning star lodged in the wall, Gladys was *strong*. Andromeda knew how to deal with that, just as she had against countless larger Watch and Royal Guard opponents during training: with agility.

"Wow, she's good," Jinny said, watching Andromeda duck and weave through Gladys's slow, powerful blows.

"She *is* my personal bodyguard for a reason," Vallora boasted.

"I meant the older one," said Jinny,

pointing to Gladys as she attempted to hack Andromeda's arm off with a hand ax. Gladys was absolutely bristling with weapons, it turned out, hidden until made to appear as if by magic. Jinny swooned. "What a lady!"

Gladys yelled, "I ain't no lady!" at the same time Andromeda shouted, "I'm *definitely* older than her!"

"Should we... do something?" Reed asked.

"Best not to interfere," said Vallora. "Andromeda can be *quite* competitive."

"Ah, as can Gladdy. Let's not, then."

The three of them rotated slowly as the fight wound around the oval-shaped cabin. Jinny occasionally glanced out the front windows and adjusted the wheel, but it was Sabah at the main navigational controls who was actually keeping them afloat.

There was plenty of open air to sail through. They'd rocketed away from Nonigate, the enormous citadel disappearing in the magical rear-view mirrors. Unfortunately, Zenith sat smack dab in the middle of a very tall mountain range, and they were not yet high enough to clear all the peaks and ridges. After demolishing a tree against the nose of the ship, Jinny whipped her attention back to the helm. It was *so* difficult to steer while two beautiful women were having a vicious blade fight all around her.

"Hang on!" Jinny shouted as she spun the wheel to avoid another sudden uprising of land in front of them.

The cabin lurched. Everyone but Jinny and Sabah, with their cat-like reflexes, took a bit of a tumble. A couple of crewmates stumbled in through the interior hall, paws braced against the doorframe, and stared wide-eyed, ears perked, at the scene before them. The wind whistling through the open exterior door was most disconcerting.

"Captain?" said one of them.

"Yes?" Jinny trilled, and at the same time, Andromeda managed a breathless, "*WHAT?*"

"Oh, I meant…" said the crewmember, but Andromeda was already busy fending off more flying knives from Gladys, knocking three of them out of the air with angled hits from her sword. Neither woman had managed to land a blow yet.

"Don't worry!" Jinny said to her crew as she maneuvered through the field of tiny islands. "It's all under control! Just keep the engine running hot!"

"That's the trouble," said Karima. She was the ship's main mechanic. They had quite a few on board, because Jinny tended to be reckless and repairs were often needed in the middle of a run. "The engine's, um, a bit *too* hot—"

The ship lurched again, but this time it wasn't because Jinny spun the wheel. It was more of a forward stutter and start. The engineers gripped the doorway. Jinny and Sabah gripped the controls. Reed clung to his lute and was thrown against Vallora's legs, which might as well have been made of steel. Vallora stayed standing.

Gladys and Andromeda smacked against the windshield and then flopped back onto the floor as the ship righted itself. Gladys was on her feet in an instant, throwing her hand ax with deadly accuracy. Andromeda did several backwards somersaults to get away, leaving the ax quivering in the plush magenta carpet.

"—we need to slow down!" Engineer Karima finished. "Or at least stop making so many sharp turns! You're pushing her too hard right out of dock!"

Jinny looked to Vallora. "Where are we headed? Which way should I go?"

"Well, I was planning to go to Savor in Revel first," Vallora said, "but I think we need to drop the Captain off in Zenith before we go. Andromeda, that is, not you."

"I'm. Not. Leaving. Without. YOU! Your! Highness!" Andromeda bit out each word as she and Gladys once again clashed blades. Her arms were tiring, but Gladys seemed to keep on coming, as strong as ever. Just *where* did she get her stamina from?

"Seems like our plans are at odds with each other, Captain," Vallora said. "I hate to play the royalty card, but I *could* order you to—"

"Not while your life is in imminent danger," Andromeda said, ducking behind Sabah. ("Now that ain't sportin'," said Gladys, "using a meat shield.") "Which it clearly is, in this company, aboard this ship. In that case, my oath expressly allows me to override any of your royal commands in the service of delivering you to safety."

"Hmm, it does, doesn't it," said Vallora thoughtfully.

*You're not at all surprised*, thought Reed, glancing up at Vallora's amused expression. *It's almost as if you meant for her to come after us—and to nearly succeed. But you're The Hero. There's no way even the best Royal Guard could beat you in a fight, even a fight of wits, isn't that right?*

At this point they'd circled desoil from nine o'clock to one o'clock around the rim of of Zenith. There would be other guard ships on their tail soon enough—Reed could see commercial and personal vessels through the wide windshield, some of them a bit too close for comfort. The cryscom crackled with incoming hails and worried requests for air channel clearance.

Jinny spun the wheel. Everyone but the crew and Vallora took another tumble.

"I'll drop you off at my house! As a fellow captain, you deserve that much," Jinny told Andromeda, who had fallen into Sabah and was springing away, red-faced, from the pretty panthera woman as if she'd been burned.

Jinny, being a descendant of an original Party member, lived in District Twelve, also known as Duodecast Hill. It sat right behind the castle and was broken into three long, skinny estates, each of which was practically a small town unto itself. The three noble families lived in opulent Upper Circumference estates while their staff were given identical rowhomes in the Lower. There was no Middle Circumference here. All the better to ensure the way things were kept working, well, like clockwork.

Unsurprisingly, the Party aristocracy had their own personal air docks. All three docks were of strikingly different architectural styles, and housed within them strikingly different styles of airships. The Silverclaws preferred rosy sandstone that would soak up warmth, big arched windows to let in enormous sunbeams for lounging, and plenty of climbing foliage and colorful waving pendants to add visual interest.

Their airships on the other hand were sleek and fast. Expensive, even more so than *My Daring Darling*. In truth, Jinny had been given her particular ship with its commercial class—she was told it would be her job in the family business to deliver goods and merchandise which could absolutely not wait on a slower ship—in part so that she would dock it elsewhere. Jinny had been learning, illegally (though what was illegality to someone who could pay the fines or pay off the judge without a thought?), to fly since she was fourteen. It was well known among staff and family that despite this, she was… not terribly *good* at it.

But all she had ever wanted to be was an airship captain. So, here she was, hovering precariously above the Silverclaw docks, absentmindedly sticking her tongue out as she tried to angle *My Daring Darling* between her mother's Marble Maven and her cousin's Beryl Buster.

Luckily, she didn't need to dock. It was at this moment, with the ship finally staying still for more than a minute, that Gladys and Andromeda found themselves all the way back by the airlock. Gladys wrenched her morning star from the wall and brandished it menacingly.

"I told you, next time it'd be your head

that gets smashed," she growled.

For the first time all day, Vallora looked genuinely worried. She reached out a gloved hand and winced. "Gladys, please go easy. Captain Stagge isn't just my guard, she's my best friend."

Andromeda heard this and felt as if the world had dropped out from under her. Then she realized it had; she'd taken a step backwards *straight* out of the open airlock. Her mind warred between two thoughts: *I'm going to die now,* and *Vallora considers me her BEST FRIEND? We're FRIENDS?*

She did not die. She *did* hit the solar sail of the boarding glider with enough velocity to knock the wind from her lungs. Her sword bounced off and fell somewhere far, far below. All she could do was stare up at the hovering, fish-like shape of *My Daring Darling*. Someone was leaning out from the airlock, the grappling hook cable in hand.

It was Vallora. Andromeda would recognize that beefy silhouette anywhere, even with stars dancing around her vision. Vallora had, with her uncanny strength and even more uncanny luck, pulled the glider into position to catch her. To save her life.

*But now yours is in danger, Your Highness,* Andromeda thought as her vision darkened. *I know it is. I don't trust any of those people on that ship. I have to bring you home. No matter what the cost.*

# 11

## Bready or Not

Once they were far away enough from Zenith, Jinny slowed the ship and turned on the cruise control. Which simply meant that Sabah took the helm, leaning her fluffy black paws across the wheel as if she hadn't a care in the world. As if the cabin around her hadn't just been shredded and dented by battle. Sabah had been hired by the Silverclaw matrons for her unshakable temperament, and to ensure that her teenage charge did not get into too much trouble.

This, Sabah thought, probably crossed a

line somewhere. Not with the fight—there'd been fights on *My Daring Darling* before—but Emperor Vallora's presence might be a problem. She wasn't sure yet. The Silverclaws were Party descendants. It seemed narratively right that Jinny, bearing the same name as her world-saving ancestor, might end up in the company of The Hero.

But something was off. She couldn't put her finger on it, watching the little group as they huddled around Gladys on the viewing sofa, making plans for their adventure. It wasn't even that Gladys and Reed were clearly shady as all hells. That only seemed right for a story like this, as far as she understood stories. Sabah had been raised in the Lower Circumference of Duodecast Hill, in a family that had been serving House Silverclaw for decades. She'd been fed all the GONE-approved tales, every book's spine stamped with their literal seal of approval.

She'd also heard things that contradicted the official stance on The Hero's journey, and all the ways the Empire had shaped the world. Things that had been whispered from generation to generation, things that had been seen while working near to the castle or within its walls, conversations overheard between Party descendants, scenes which could not be *un*seen.

Sabah's tail swished. She watched Vallora, whom she'd only ever seen from afar before now. She thought maybe Vallora was the one to keep an eye on.

Well, Sabah deserved to have a little fun, didn't she? Even if she was a side character barely worth naming, much less given a full backstory and development arc. *Especially* if she was expected to lay down her life for the Captain and her 'more important' companions.

If it came to that, Sabah would contact the Silverclaws for assistance. She was not so won over by the Empire that she'd sacrifice herself for it.

Reed noticed her watching, but said nothing. He understood already that though Jinny bore the title of Captain, that Sabah was the one in charge here. Things were often like that when it came to positions of power, whether it was airship crews, Empire politicians, or the ranks of the resistance itself. If they stayed aboard this ship for very long, he'd have to test Sabah to see who she would ultimately lend her power to.

Reed could be very persuasive when he wanted to be.

"I'm gonna have bruises up m'whole arms for weeks," Gladys complained, lounging across all three pink velvet seats. Other than the scowl on her face, she seemed no worse for wear after facing down Andromeda.

"Sorry about that," Vallora said. "I know some good healing spells, if you'd like?"

Gladys hugged her skinny arms to her chest. "I would not."

"Don't worry about her, she's tough as stale camel jerky," Reed said, kicking the base of the couch. "More liable to break the teeth chewing on her than get chewed up."

Vallora turned her curious gaze on him. "And you? Are you all right, Mr. Thorley?"

Reed was surprised to find that he felt a bit shaken. Not afraid, but riled up, rattled, ready to fight, even if his weapon of choice was words rather than fists or blades. More energy coursed through his veins than ever had in the past few decades. He gave Vallora a crooked grin.

"Suppose so, Your Highness," he said.

Vallora pulled a face. "Now, don't start calling me that."

"Then don't call me 'Mr. Thorley.'"

"Understood."

Jinny, who had been mooning over Gladys, looked up curiously, her paws pressed together in front of her chest. She held one of them out to Reed. "Then what *are* you called? I'm Captain Jindra Silverclaw the Thirty-Sixth, but everyone calls me Jinny."

Reed took her hand gingerly. Her paw pads were soft from a short lifetime of luxury. Reed was over the hill now, as they said, past fifty, and the nineteen-year-old panthera seemed to him a ridiculous baby, even if she was technically an adult.

She reminded him a bit of himself, years and years ago. Years and years.

"Just Reed is fine," he said. "Pleasure to meet you."

Ginny giggled and said, "All right, Just Reed, pleasure to meet you too," with a wink.

Reed kicked the couch again and said, "This is Gladdy."

Gladys bolted upright indignantly.

"Don't you *dare*."

Jinny gave her a deep, regal bow. "I would never! A woman as strong and brave as yourself deserves only to be called by the most respected of names!"

Gladys's indignation melted away instantly. She puffed out her chest and tossed her braid over her shoulder, head tilted at what she thought was a noble angle. "They call me Gladys the Destroyer."

"From the Hundred Mile Waste, Bandit Queen of the Banded Canyon, slayer of the High Road Highwayman," recited Vallora, once again echoing the exact cadence Reed had used in the pub.

Gladys crossed her arms and squinted at Vallora. She gave Jinny a softer look normally reserved only for her son. Which was only about as soft as gravel, but it made a difference. "*You* can just call me Gladys."

Jinny went starry-eyed at this. Reed marveled at the way the old woman could make loyal, instant fans of anyone who saw her fight. It was rather like the reaction he and his bandmates had gotten when they were Jinny's age, any time they opened their mouths to sing, or even just *appeared*, given their rakishly good looks. Perhaps it was a good thing that marketing agents and managers in Hextory didn't know what they were missing with this particular demographic.

An awkward silence fell, filled only by airship ambiance. A low hum. The background radiation of the crystal core, like a cup of tea you'd forgotten to finish and a once-roaring forge banked down to embers.

"So," said Reed, "shall we go to Savor?"

"Yes!" said Vallora.

"Why Savor?"

Vallora blinked. "They've got good farms. Best bread I ever had, I had in Savor. I'd like to have it again. I might have lied initially about my identity, but I was serious about going on a food tour of the world."

Jinny put her hands on her hips. "A food tour! That's the adventure we're going on?"

She sounded a little put out, and indeed that was how she felt. When Vallora appeared on her ship and asked her to join the adventure, then instructed her to lie to Gate Control and illegally exit Zenith at high speed, pursued by the Royal Guard, she'd imagined much higher stakes were afoot.

Vallora patted her shoulder. "We'll be pursued. I've only thrown off Captain Stagge for a moment. I know her, and she won't stop until she catches us. We'll be undercover, and certainly relying on more of your excellent flying, to make sure that doesn't happen until I want it to."

Jinny looked mollified. Especially by the compliment on her flying.

"Y'plan on going back?" Gladys asked, surprised.

It was as if a curtain had dropped over Vallora's face. The bright, sunny expression there dimmed to nothing. She looked like a statue carved from dark stone.

"I don't think I have any other choice," she said. "I do take my responsibilities to the Empire seriously. I'll have to return to them at some point."

Everyone thought, but no one said, *Then why did you have to escape from them the way that you did? Why couldn't you simply make a few royal decrees and taste the cuisine of the world in style, welcomed with fanfare everywhere you went? You could have commanded that the trip be a quiet, secret affair, if that's the problem? Royals do whatever they want. That's the very nature of royalty.*

Of course they each thought this in their own particular dialect and idiom. Gladys largely thought in concepts and pictures rather than words, and was tainted by deep suspicion of everyone and everything. Jinny had just about every thought simultaneously, in one chaotic tangle bundle tinged by confusion over what seemed to her to be common sense.

Reed thought these thoughts just about exactly as written. Sabah was not very far off. What *Vallora* was actually thinking was a complete mystery to everyone on board.

"Well, then," Reed said, "to Savor! And the best bread in the world!"

# 12

## Not The End Without Friends

Andromeda was angry. She was also in pain, which made her more angry. Yes, Vallora had saved her life, and she'd be forever grateful for that, even though it was *Vallora's* fault she was on board *My Daring Darling* in the first place. It was *Vallora's* fault she had to open the airlock with the emergency lever, which meant it wouldn't close properly.

But *Andromeda* was the one who had failed. As a result, she had a cracked rib, Vallora was gone, and Commander Haywood was berating her for not calling in backup first thing this morning, when she'd found the note.

After she passed out, House Silverclaw staff had anchored the boarding glider and taken her to a room to recover. They'd removed her armor and set the house healer on her. She regained consciousness with the mage staring *straight* into her eyeballs at a distance close enough to count his nose hairs. She'd panicked and sat up too fast, smacking their heads together hard enough to see stars a second time that day.

"Well, if you didn't already have a concussion, you might now," the healer had groaned. "At least you're mobile, I suppose."

She did not have a concussion. The healer wrapped her chest, gave her a bone healing tonic that tasted like black licorice, and told her not to exert herself for the next week. Andromeda did not verbally agree to this, as she had no plans to comply. She would be exerting herself. Probably quite a lot. Her body, which had a high level of pain tolerance anyway, would just have to deal.

Two of Captain Jinny's mothers had

come to see if she was all right. The third one was out at a costume party in Hendecary. Panthera women raised their children communally, with any number of parents, unlike the two most elves had. Jindra Silverclaw the Thirty-Fifth and Sultana Silverclaw were kind, if a little too physically touchy for Andromeda's taste. They were also extremely nosy, demanding as many details as Andromeda was willing to give about her strange appearance in their residence, and what it had to do with their daughter's ship.

Andromeda thought they should have been horrified by Jinny's exploits. Instead they laughed and said they *knew* Jinny would have an exciting destiny, given she had the very same fur coloration as the original Jindra Silverclaw. It was as if they were expecting this to happen.

Which Andromeda had to admit, made a lot of sense. Would-be heroic companions *were* often found by significant birthmarks, scars, or resemblance to someone famous from the past.

Then Commander Haywood had come. She'd had to repeat the story all over again, then endure even more intense questioning about the details. Andromeda was exhausted and sore from her fight with Gladys, not to mention from falling out of an airship, but that was no excuse. She was Captain of the Royal Guard. She would bear her fatigue and pain and she would bear them with dignity.

What *really* distracted her from the Commander's tirade was this: Vallora's last words before Andromeda tumbled from the airlock. Over and over again, in her mind. *She's my best friend. She's my best friend. She's my best friend. She's my best friend.*

*If I'm your best friend,* Andromeda thought moodily, *then why did you leave me behind?*

Haywood stopped pacing and snapped his fingers in front of her face. Andromeda scowled at him, and he scowled back.

"Captain, are you even listening?" he demanded.

"Yes," she said, "sir."

"Sometimes I can't tell with you," said Haywood. "It's good to shield your emotions and look uninterested as a guard to throw off the enemy, but *really.*"

Andromeda wondered if Haywood knew

that she considered *him* the enemy. The Commander was an satyr with charcoal-colored fur, pale skin, and blazing yellow eyes. His horns were enormous black spirals that he kept polished with some kind of oil. On the tips he wore little golden caps with sharpened points. He was tall and brutishly strong, intimidating to all but the most foolish. Even Gladys would have admitted he had a fearsome look, especially when dressed in battle armor.

Commander Haywood was always dressed in battle armor. Commander Haywood also treated Vallora like a weapon rather than a living being. Like a magic canon that could be aimed wherever the Empire needed it, regardless of the canon's personal thoughts, feelings, or health. Vallora was always cordial, even kind in return, never appearing to take the commander's objectification to heart.

So Andromeda, in *her* heart, was offended on Vallora's behalf. She'd never said so aloud, not to Haywood's face, no. But she *had* perhaps been more obstinate than necessary with him, had occasionally complied with his orders in such a literal fashion as to be malicious in execution.

He had yet to catch her in the act in the thirty years she'd been Captain. But he *was* suspicious.

Andromeda had no patience for that game now. She glared at him until he gave her a bit more space. She swung her legs over the side of the bed, grateful she was still wearing pants, and began collecting her armor from where it sat on the bedside table.

"Don't worry," she said, "I'm going after her. Immediately."

Haywood snorted derisively. No one snorted derisively like a satyr.

"What, alone?" he asked. "In whose ship? With what provisions? Weapons? Traps? Have you even got a plan, Stagge?"

"I know Her Highness best," Andromeda said, tightening her bracers. Gladys had left quite a few scratches and dents in the metal. She'd have to have them looked after. "I know how she thinks, what she enjoys, where she's likely to go. I will find her and bring her back safe. It's my duty."

Haywood picked up one of her shin guards and held it out of her reach like a playground bully. He examined the damage from being thrown around the ship and shook his head.

"You tried that already, Captain. You failed. Perhaps," he said, "someone *else* should go, while you think about the consequences you'll face for your mistakes. Several someones, I think, a small platoon with a warship, or—"

"No warships. Not for this."

Haywood and Andromeda turned to the doorway at the sound of Tansy's voice. Haywood bowed, and Andromeda got to her feet to do the same. It made her cracked rib twinge. Tansy gestured for them to be at ease and glided into the room, closing the door behind her tightly.

The Empress was dressed just as plainly as she had been earlier, except she was now wearing a gold circlet around her brow. She held herself straighter. With those two changes, Tansy could never be mistaken for anyone *but* the Empress of the Unending Empire. There was just that kind of aura about her. The same strange aura of Destiny that hung around Vallora. And, well, around Destiny, the Dog.

Andromeda wondered where the Dog had gotten off to after being left in the Nonigate control tower. The mutt could absolutely find her own way home, but that didn't mean she wasn't having herself a garbage can feast on the way back, which would leave her stinking and farting for days. Likely in Andromeda's company.

Tansy smiled, but a couple of tears gathered in the corners of her downturned eyes. Andromeda couldn't help but picture the comic makeup the players had used for Tansy's face in their Backstage performance. It was eerily accurate, in a way. Especially for people who likely had never seen the Empress in person, except perhaps atop a holiday parade float.

Tansy did what she could for orphans and the like, it was true. Zenith was an enormous city, the largest on the planet, and so she would never be truly known to all of her subjects. Still, they had her essence down pat.

Tansy looked slowly at each of them and said, "Lora is a bit too clever for her own good sometimes. Or the good of the Empire. Force will not work. Trickery will not work. The only way to get Lora to do anything is if she thinks she *wants* to do it."

Haywood snorted again. "Apologies,

Your Highness. Of course you're right. *You* know the Emperor best, after all."

Andromeda missed a lot of tonal cues in spoken language, but she didn't miss *that* one.

"No apologies necessary," Tansy sighed.

She approached the bed and took Andromeda's hands in hers. Tansy's hands were small and gentle, just like the rest of her. Magical warmth flooded through Andromeda's body, erasing her pain and renewing her energy. Andromeda felt as if she could run the length of the entire Rim and not be winded. She wasn't even hungry, and she'd barely eaten anything all day. Tansy's eyes flashed gold, and then the spell was over. No runes or chanting or ritual gestures. Just a simple touch. That's how powerful the Empress was.

"Go," said Tansy. "Go, and don't come back unless Lora is with you. Whatever it takes. I love Lora, and I know you do, too. Neither of us can truly rest until we know she's home, safe from those Antihero anarchists. If they get a hold of Lora, they'll experiment on her and put her to death. That's what they've always said, and you and I know they now have the means. I can't even bear to think of it, can you? What it would *do* to the world, to lose their Hero? *Our* Hero?"

Andromeda nodded jerkily. *I love Lora, and I know you do, too.* Did Tansy know that Andromeda pined after her wife, or did she assume they shared the same platonic feelings of deep friendship? Andromeda had heard Tansy encourage Vallora to seek out a new romantic partner—albeit one kept secret from the public—but she'd never indicated that Andromeda might be a good candidate.

Beyond her surface-level kindness, Tansy's true intentions remained unreadable, as always.

"I will succeed," Andromeda forced herself to say. "I swear it to you and to the Empire."

The two tears loitering in Tansy's eyes fell silently down her face. She squeezed Andromeda's hands. "I believe in you, Captain. And so does Vallora."

TO BE CONTINUED IN:

# Adventurers Kneaded

## Empire of Eats Novella #2

Emperor Vallora and her new Party are officially on the run! The first stop on their cozy worldwide food tour is none other than the city of Savor, where Vallora once ate the best bread she'd ever had in her 900-year-old life. Only, when they arrive on the famous Ovenue (that's "oven" plus "avenue), there's only sawdust and sadness to be found. It turns out the local nobility are hoarding all the best wheat flour for themselves—and a few other, more worrying things besides.

Captain Andromeda follows with the intention of returning Vallora home to Zenith Castle, but first, she finds her very particular palate being used as a taste-tester for noble ale brewers. Will she ever get the bitter taste of hops, wealth, and status out of her mouth? Something odd is going on behind the walls of the Solstice Dam, and it has to do with airship engines as much as local agriculture. Whether Andromeda has time to investigate a new mystery on top of stopping Vallora's attempt to break a rebel out of prison is up to her…

**Coming Fall 2024**

# Other Great Books From the Kraken Collective!

AWAKENINGS: The Chronicles of Nerezia 1

If you want more novellas with rich queer worlds that combine the fun warmth of cozy fantasy with the exciting tropes of large JRPGs and epic fantasy, try *Awakenings* by Claudie Arseneault, in which an enthusiastic embo (e/em himbo) embarks in a magical Wagon to help eir amnesiac elven friend find the mystical grove of their dreams.

*Awakenings* is the first of nine novellas, all imbued with an aspec-focused queernormative world and strong platonic bonds.

**More information, books, and buy links can be found at:**
https://www.krakencollectivebooks.com/books/awakenings

# Find more of Cedar McCloud's work and stay in touch with new and upcoming releases!

*Cedar McCloud is a queer, auDHD disabled artist and author living in southern California with their partner and cat. They enjoy archaic crafts, nature walks, food, and fashion, despite not being any good at that last one. They use storytelling as a tool for trauma healing and self-expression, which sounds serious but is sometimes pretty goofy in practice. Cedar is a professional Tarot illustrator, lazy witch, and full-time magical being.*

**Website**
numinousspiritpress.com

**Instagram**
instagram.com/numinousspirit

**Newsletter**
numinousspiritpress.com/newsletter

Newsletters are sent 1-2 times per month and include progress on current and upcoming works, availability and special sales, and occasional blog posts about life, writing, and art. You can check out examples of past newsletters on the **blog**: numinousspiritpress.com/blog

# Author's Note

This novella is the result of many, many years of *saying* I wanted to write something comedic, getting very invested in an idea, and ultimately never finishing the manuscript in question. I'm glad to finally put something funny out into the world! I grew up being known as the "serious friend," so it means a lot that I'm able to share my goofy side with folks now, however weird and off-beat it may be. I hope you all have a little laugh, and I hope you have some delicious comfort foods you can snack on during or after reading this book.

As an ever-present reminder, autism is a huge spectrum, and every autistic person is unique. Andromeda's experiences are based on my own, and can't represent everyone in the community. It's important to remember that we all have different traits, strengths, and areas of support. If you really relate to characters like Andromeda and think you might be autistic, check out the #ActuallyAutistic hashtag on your favorite social media platform and see if you find other folks there whose personal, internal experiences you resonate with.

An enormous thank you, as always, to my writer friends for their support, especially S.L. Dove and Claudie Arsenault, who I chat with about books on a daily basis. Claudie especially was a crucial partner in helping bring this new series to life, as we both were struck by the inspiration to write a JRPG-inspired fantasy series right around the same time, and spent a lot of fun hours brainstorming together!

Thank you as well to the Kraken Collective for taking me into the fold, as I know from experience that indie creators are stronger when we stand together in support. I'm honored to be among so many talented authors, many of whose books I loved long before joining.

A similar thank you to Jeanna Kadlec's Astrology for Writers Discord server, where there are so many awesome and cool folks ready to discuss not just the writing process, but also the particulars of our birth charts and the astro-weather for the day. You've all provided such a lovely community space to play around in. And of course, Jeanna's Astrology for Writers Substack has been a wonderful companion in helping me to chart my writing life alongside the stars.

Finally, the biggest thank you of all to my loving partner, Shamus, for listening to me ramble constantly about my characters and for supporting us financially while I find my feet after burnout. It means the world to me that you see the value and importance of my creative dreams and help make them possible by keeping us fed and sheltered. I love you more than I love ketchup, and you KNOW how much I love ketchup!

Happy eating!
Cedar McCloud
March 26, 2024